Mr Ted's

Police Dog

Adventures

Eddie Halling

Contents

Chapter One

Mr Ted goes to the World's End

"Stand Still now! Or I'll send the dog!" Mr Ted's ears stood up, he strained on his lead, he was barking loud and aggressively, as he always did when he heard that challenge being laid down by Constable Wood. He could see who his handler was shouting at; it was a man carrying a heavy bag in his left hand. He was running away from them across an open field. Constable Wood shouted after the man once more, before sending Ted on his way to stop him. Ted was gaining on the runaway and as he got close he leapt into the air as he launched himself at the fleeing criminal's arm.

Constable Wood looked into Ted's kennel as he went to get him for their night shift together. He could see Mr Ted lying on the floor on his side. He was asleep, but his legs were moving and he was shaking his head as he lay there.

"Come on Ted. Wake up. You're dreaming and it looks like your running after someone, judging by the way you're moving about." Ted opened his eyes straight away at the sound of Constable Wood's voice and stood up to greet him.

"Right Ted, we've got to go to work now," Constable Wood explained, as he led Ted from his kennel and got into the waiting police dog van. "Sorry to break in to your dream like that. I hope you got him whoever it was."

Mr Ted, the German Shepherd police dog, got his name because when he was born he looked just like a teddy bear, or so the farmer and his wife thought on the day he arrived, and the name stuck. It stayed with him all through his career as a police dog. It had taken three months of hard training to equip Mr Ted with the skills to be a police dog, his experience came from the patrol work that he and Constable Wood did, and the many adventures they encountered working together. They were inseparable. Mr Ted only worked with Constable Wood, and Constable Wood only worked with Mr Ted, they were partners. They were out on patrol together as usual late one autumn evening in their police patrol van. Patrolling in the van or on foot was routine business for the dog and man team, they had done it many times before and this day was much the same as most of the days that they spent on patrol, one minute all was quiet then suddenly and unexpectedly the silence inside the patrolling police van was broken by a radio message coming from the police headquarters. They were calling Constable Wood and Mr Ted, whose radio call sign was Alpha 41. The control room had used that call sign to contact them and send them to the World's End mini market in Newtown Street in Hawkridge, because the burglar alarm had gone off.

No one knew why it was called The World's End, it just was. It wasn't anywhere near the end of the world, wherever that is, it was just on one corner of an ordinary residential street in Hawkridge. The shop had been broken into several times before; it was always late in the evening or in the night, when it was closed for business. The thieves always stole money from the till, if there was any there, and alcohol from the display shelves. They always caused damage as they broke into the shop and pulled things from the shelves. This was the third time in a month that the shop had

6

been attacked and no one had ever been caught for it. Constable Wood knew that as he answered the radio.

"We're not far away; we'll be there in a couple of minutes." he told the control room operator.

He switched on the blue light on top the van and sped off towards the World's End. Mr Ted had been through this before, and he knew he was on his way to a task that would need his training and skills. He sensed the urgency in Constable Wood's driving, and the sound of the electric motor of the blue police light turning round and round on the roof above him, confirmed that they were going to the scene of a crime. Mr Ted became more alert than usual, wondering to himself what it was that they were speeding to in such a hurry. He barked with excitement as they drove along, looking out of the windows at the back and front of the van taking in everything that he could see and hear.

Moments later Constable Wood pulled up in the street, a few metres away from the front of the World's End shop. He got out of the van and, taking Mr Ted with him on his lead, they walked together on the pavement on the opposite side to the shop.

"Quiet now Ted. There's burglars at work here I think. I might need you to catch them in a minute."

Everything looked as it should. The shop was closed for business and the lights inside the shop were all off. The only light visible was the light that lit up the sign above the door. There was no noise at all as the pair reached the front door, there were no burglar alarm bells sounding. Constable Wood expected that, it was because they were designed to ring only at the police station and not at the shop, so if any burglars were there they would not know that the police had been called.

Constable Wood pushed against the door and tried the handle, but it was locked firmly shut. Mr Ted looked up at Constable Wood, and looked back at the shop doorway again. He was excited and keen to get on with his job, but up to now he couldn't see what the job was. He kept quiet as Constable Wood stepped back away from the door to look up and down the street and then through the glass display window to see if there was any movement from inside. What he could see was darkness, and the glow of a small standby light on the freezer against the back wall of the shop. He stepped back out onto the road again and looked at the whole width of the shop, down one side he noticed an alleyway that led to the back. It was as black as a witch's hat on Halloween inside the alley and he couldn't see to the other end, but to get to the back of the shop he and Mr Ted needed to go along it, and so they did. With Mr Ted at his side on his lead, Constable Wood walked slowly into the darkness leaving the friendly glow of the street lighting behind them as it got darker and darker in the tunnel-like alley way.

After they had walked a few metres Mr Ted, walked one or two paces in front of Constable Wood, as dogs nearly always are when you take them out on a lead, he suddenly came to a stop. Something was blocking his way, but the policeman couldn't see what it was. Mr Ted could see it, and he knew he couldn't get through it without Constable Wood's help. Constable Wood took another pace to get alongside Mr Ted. He put his right hand out in front of him, into the darkness, and touched a wooden gate, a solid wooden gate that stood two metres high. As he touched it the gate began to slowly open, its hinges creaking eerily in the darkness as it did so, then it fell inwards and off one of its hinges, making a noise of wood hitting concrete as it did so.

"We could do without making noises like that Ted. I hope the burglar didn't hear us!"

Constable Wood and Mr Ted stepped through the gate slowly, carefully and deliberately, not knowing what they might discover on the other side. Suddenly from above Constable Wood, there came a loud scream and something heavy dropped on him landing on his right shoulder: he felt the pain of a dozen sharp spikes digging into him from whatever it was that landed so heavily on his shoulder. Then it dropped to the ground beside him. Constable Wood's heart was thumping at the suddenness of this unexpected attack from above; as he looked down he could see nothing but darkness. Mr Ted stiffened his muscles and jumped at the sound of the screech. He pulled Constable Wood backwards on the lead back along the alleyway to the street, after the dark shadow that he could see running in front of him. He could see what it was and he was going after it! The policeman had trouble restraining the big German Shepherd, and keeping his balance at the same time: it all happened so quickly as they charged towards the street after a shadow in the dark! Constable Wood regained his balance just as they got to the pavement. Mr Ted was looking to his left along the

10

road, and as Constable Wood followed his gaze he saw what Mr Ted could see - a big black tom cat running along the road!

"Leave him Ted. Let's get on with this alarm call shall we?" Eddie said quietly. "We don't need any more stunts like that if we're ever going to see what's going on inside here."

The pair walked back along the alleyway into the yard at the back of the shop. Constable Wood stood on some broken glass outside the back door: he was careful to make sure that Mr Ted didn't step into it and cut his unprotected paws. He and Mr Ted looked through the broken glass window at the back of the shop. They couldn't see anything at first, but then, in the darkness, they saw a flicker of a torch light inside, a sure sign that burglars were at work. Constable Wood tried the handle and the door opened inwards. As he and Mr Ted entered the doorway they were just in time to see two men letting themselves out of the front door onto the street and run off. Constable Wood and Mr Ted ran through the shop after them and out onto the pavement. They saw them both disappearing along the street ahead of them.

"Stand still or I will release the police dog!" shouted Constable Wood.

Mr Ted was straining at the lead, ready to go and barking! He could see his target running away from him; he wanted to be released from his lead to do his job.

"Stand still NOW!"

The two men looked back at them and carried on running but looked long enough to see Constable Wood reach down and release Mr Ted from his lead with his left hand.

"Stop them!"

Mr Ted took off at lightning speed; he was super fit and trained to catch criminals in situations like this. The two burglars stood no chance against Mr Ted, there was no way they could out run him, and they couldn't hide either. They were on borrowed time now.

The fleeing criminals turned the corner at the end of the street, ahead of them they saw another two police constables walking towards them, and when they looked back they saw a massive police dog bearing down on them.

Constable Wood shouted again, "Stand perfectly still-NOW!" The two men stopped where they were just as Mr Ted got to within two metres of them. When he saw that they had stopped and given up, Mr Ted circled around them barking, just as he had been trained to do. As he did so, keeping them in one place until Constable Wood joined him. The two burglars were trapped, trembling with fear, holding on to each other for comfort, not wanting the barking, snarling dog to sink its teeth into their shaking bodies. The only chance they had now was to listen to everything that the policeman was shouting at them, and to make no sudden moves. The last thing they expected when they broke into the corner shop to steal was to be chased by a monster sized angry police dog.

"Ted leave!" shouted Constable Wood. Mr Ted looked briefly at his partner and stopped his barking.

"Mr Ted, Down!"

Mr Ted dropped to the ground, much to the relief of his two captives, lying still in one spot, never taking his eyes off the two of them until the two approaching policemen took them into custody. Mr Ted was ready for the men to start running again. He wanted them to run because he enjoyed the chase. But this time the two constables took one man each and arrested them. Constable Wood called Mr Ted to him; he slipped him back on to his lead and walked off back to the police van.

"Well done Ted. I said you would be needed, didn't I? You're good at catching burglars. Nobody gets away from Mr Ted."

That was another job well done by Mr Ted; he had obeyed every command from his handler. This exciting chase and arrest was indeed a job well done, but only one of hundreds of similar adventures that they would go through together. He was a well trained, well disciplined police dog, but he wasn't born a police dog. He started life just like any other dog, one of a litter each destined to go their separate ways once they had been weaned from their mother, but Ted's life was to be hugely different from that of his siblings.

Chapter Two

Early Days on the Farm

Mr Ted is a big dog by any standard, bigger even than most other German Shepherds. Black and tan in colour, kind and friendly by nature, but trained at the police dog training school to work with his handler, Police Constable Eddie Wood to catch criminals, look for missing people and search for lost and stolen property. When he is catching criminals he looks ferocious, especially when he is barking and he shows his teeth, criminals usually give up straight away when they see Mr Ted chasing after them. He wasn't always a police dog; he wasn't even born into a police dog family. In fact, Mr Ted was born on Mr and Mrs Wilson's cattle farm at Suttonbury, Walthamshire, at the same time as his five brothers and sisters. His proud Mum, a German Shepherd farm dog called Jess looked after him affectionately for the first few weeks of his life. After that he and the others started to look after themselves more and more, and didn't need her so much. They soon started running all about the farm getting into mischief exploring everything and everywhere they could get to before being rounded up again. Mr Ted loved those carefree early days. He had everything, a caring mum, brothers and sisters to play with, plenty of food and somewhere warm and friendly to sleep whenever he wanted to.

Mr Ted, because he was a pedigree dog born to pedigree parents, was registered at the kennel club with the kennel name Melward Surprise. All pedigree dogs have a kennel name as well as their every day name. He was named by Mrs Wilson because Melward was their registered kennel name and he was called *Surprise* because he arrived last in the line of the six puppies, much later than the others by a couple of hours, and everyone thought that Jess had finished having them all. So it came as a surprise to Jess and Mr and Mrs Wilson when Mr Ted was born. Not only that, but he was the smallest of the litter and looked weak and unlikely to survive his own birth. Mrs Wilson thought he had been still born when she first saw him. He didn't look like he was breathing and he was cold, but Jess worked hard to revive him by cleaning him and nudging him into life. A few anxious moments later he started to breath for himself, after a lot of attention from Jess and, apart from his very small size, he soon fitted in with the others competing for his mother's attention and milk. His dad, Bonus, also a German Shepherd wasn't too bothered about Mr Ted or any of the others. Bonus was a champion show dog and had won many awards for his good looks, temperament and ability at dog shows all around the country. He just got on with the things that dogs do all day long on a farm, looking out for strangers, eating and sleeping and making sure that Jess wasn't fed any more than him. As far as Bonus was concerned he was the top dog and wasn't going to be overshadowed by his youngest son who knew nothing about life as far as he was concerned.

After a couple of months or so, people started to come to the farm to look at the puppy dogs and one by one the puppies left to start a new life with their new owners. All that is, except Mr Ted. He was left alone with his mum and dad at the farm, and it seemed that for months no one outside the farm wanted him. He felt sad when his brothers and sisters left one after the other, but at the same time he was happy to be still with his mother and father in familiar surroundings. He was like an only child, and he was getting bigger all the time, more independent and looking more and more the most handsome specimen of a German Shepherd you will ever see. He was tall, had beautiful colours, a bushy tail that hung just right, and upright pointed ears that could hear the slightest sound no matter how far away it was. His sense of smell was perfect, just as it should be, and many times greater than any human being. He was the last of the litter to be born and he was the last to leave home.

When his first birthday arrived he was still at the farm, sometimes fighting with his dad, and sometimes running in the fields with the horses and cows. He just liked running alongside them, barking as loud as he could with excitement in his voice, enjoying every minute of his freedom, and the company of the other animals. The farmer and his wife already had two big dogs in Jess and Bonus, and no time to really look after Mr Ted properly as well. They really did not know what to do about him. He wasn't a puppy anymore; he was as big as his dad, a fully grown dog, and a bit of a handful at times. The answer came when a regular visitor to the farm to collect the milk every day, John Edwards, talked to Mrs Wilson about his liking for Mr Ted. He had watched Mr Ted grow over the past year and thought he was a handsome dog that would make a good family pet. He mentioned to Mrs Wilson that he would love to take care of Mr Ted and give him a home with his family, that's when Mr Ted was given to John Edwards, his wife and two young children to keep and look after.

When Mr Ted was taken away from the farm in John Edward's milk lorry he was confused. He couldn't understand why he was being taken from his home and his mother and all the things that he knew and loved.

Mr Ted, although he had an excellent temperament, a brave disposition and a strong will never did fit in at John the milkman's family home. He kept looking for every opportunity to run from the garden, out of the gate and along the road to the fields nearby, where he would run after the cows. Mr Ted was longing to be back at the farm. He would have gone back himself if he could have found the way, but he couldn't. The nearest he could get was to the fields nearby and run with the cows there. He ran away so many times, and spent so much time in the fields with the other animals that John Edwards became worried and concerned that he couldn't control him and that Mr Ted would one day get into serious trouble for cow chasing. He tried to train Mr Ted to stay inside the garden of his home, but no amount of training by John could keep Ted inside. He could leap over the gate in one go with the ease of an antelope jumping over a hedge, and no matter how much he was called he would defiantly disobey any call to come back and run off to the fields, as happy and contented as a dog could be at the thought of joining the other animals in a game of chase, where he did all the chasing.

John Edwards, despite all his trying, never could control Mr Ted. He loved him dearly, but following a family conference they all agreed that Mr Ted had to go for his own sake and safety. Just by chance John heard an appeal on the local BBC radio station which was made by the police. They were looking for young active dogs to recruit as police dogs. Preferably German Shepherd dogs with a good temperament, and in good health. With his handsome good looks, size, stamina and good temperament, Mr Ted seemed to fit the bill. John Edwards rang the Walthamshire Police Dog Section sergeant and offered Mr Ted to the police. From that moment on, although he didn't know it then, Mr Ted's life was to change beyond all recognition, for the better!

Sergeant Fleming, the police dog section sergeant, arranged an appointment with John Edwards for a police dog handler to visit him and Mr Ted at his home so that an assessment could be made as to his suitability as a police dog. Police Constable Eddie Wood met Mr Ted for the first time one sunny afternoon. When he arrived at the house John Edwards opened the door and Mr Ted ran straight past him, seizing his opportunity for freedom. He looked at Constable Wood as he passed him on the drive and let out an excited bark as if to say hello to the policeman. He wasn't running away from the police, he didn't know anything about the police. What attracted him more than anything else was the smell of the fields, and his friends the cows. Off he went not looking back once even though John Edwards was shouting embarrassedly after him to come back. The last thing John needed was for Mr Ted to escape right in front of the policeman, especially when he was hoping that the policeman might take him. He thought he had blown his chances as Mr Ted disappeared down the road out of control. Constable Wood said

"I suppose that's him is it?"

"I'll go and get him" said John Edwards hopefully, running off after Mr Ted calling his name to no avail.

What an embarrassment Mr Ted was now, just when he should have been on his best behaviour. After some chasing around the field John Edwards finally got hold of Mr Ted, and while he was trying to catch him Constable Wood was looking at the way Mr Ted moved, ran, changed direction and the way he walked. He liked what he saw. He thought that Mr Ted certainly looked the part, even if he had no training at all at the moment. In fact, he thought, it's better if Mr Ted has had no training, it will make him easier to train as a police dog; we can start from the beginning with no bad habits built in.

John Edwards led Mr Ted by his collar back to the waiting policeman, after looking Mr Ted in the eye Constable Wood allowed him to smell the back of his hand before making a real fuss of him. Mr Ted responded to Eddie with affection and displayed his feelings at meeting the policeman by wagging his tail as fast as a pair of helicopter rotor blades. They liked each other, Mr Ted liked the firm kind voice of authority, and Eddie Wood liked Mr Ted's size, good looks and temperament.

An agreement was struck in writing between Police Constable Eddie Wood and John Edwards about Mr Ted's future, and ownership of Mr Ted passed to the police there and then that day. Although John and his family were sorry to see him go, they knew he would be well cared for, and hoped that he would enjoy his new life in the police.

"Bring him back to see us one day please." said Mrs Edwards as Mr Ted walked away with Constable Wood. Mr Ted was happy enough to go with the policeman. He seemed kind and Mr Ted liked the way he spoke to him.

Of course, you don't get to be a police dog just by being a German Shepherd who looks the part; months of formal training with Police Constable Eddie Wood lay ahead of Mr Ted at the police dog training school at the Southdown Police Headquarters, Mount Browne, Gapford.

Chapter Three

Starting a Career in the Police

As they left John Edward's home PC Wood put Mr Ted onto a lead and led him to the waiting police dog van out in the street. Mr Ted looked back with fondest in his eyes at the family who were waving him goodbye. PC Wood opened the back door to the large caged area and invited Mr Ted to get in. "Get up Ted" said PC Wood. Instinctively Mr Ted looked up at him, with a knowing look in his eyes, and jumped up into the van as PC Wood touched the van floor to encourage him. The policeman closed the door and could see Mr Ted looking out with bright happy eyes, and his tail wagging. "Get up Ted" was the first real command that PC Wood had given to Ted, and he was going to hear a lot of that, and more like it, in the weeks ahead of him.

They drove off to the Walthamshire Police dog kennels about fifteen miles away in the small market town of Wavehill in the centre of the county, which was surrounded by parkland, ideal for dog walking and exercising. Police dogs and their handlers could often be seen in the park exercising every day. Police Constable Eddie Wood led Mr Ted on his lead from the van to a block of kennels built of red brick topped by an iron bar fence. Each kennel, and there were eight of them, had an entrance gate which led into its own long, open exercise area, which in turn led to a red brick dog kennel with electric light and heating.

Mr Ted was led into a kennel that was set aside for him, and would be his home for a while. He was greeted by the barking of more German Shepherds, some of the other kennels had some trained police dogs in them, and they made sure that Mr Ted knew that they were around, and that they were there before him. All the barking and the strange surroundings made Mr Ted feel a bit nervous. PC Wood shouted "Quiet!" and all the dogs, without exception, stopped barking, watching Mr Ted and his handler as they went into the empty kennel. PC Wood spent some minutes with Mr Ted to make sure he was comfortable at being left in the kennel exercise area. He wanted Mr Ted to feel comfortable there, but he knew that leaving him alone in these strange surroundings might be difficult for him at first. He gave him a bowl of water and closed the gate behind him as he left Ted alone. He wrote Mr Ted's name on the gate and it read "Trainee Police Dog Mr Ted."

"You'd better get some rest Mr Ted, you're going to the vets tomorrow, and he is going to give you the once over."

Mr Ted settled down for the night as best he could, interrupted by other police dogs and handlers coming in and out of the kennels all through the night as they were called to their work. Every time there was some movement he jumped up looking for someone to come and talk to him, but there was no work for Ted yet, not until he was trained.

The next day, early in the morning, Police Constable Wood came into the kennel block; Mr Ted looked very pleased to see him at last as he took him on the lead to the nearby parkland and went for a long walk around the park. Ted was never let off the lead once, and wouldn't be until he had passed his training, and Constable Wood could be sure that he wouldn't run off like he did at John Edward's home. Even so, Mr Ted enjoyed the walk and being with Constable Wood, just as much as the policeman enjoyed his dogs company. When they got back to the kennels Mr Ted was treated to a full grooming by PC Wood and then a bowl of fresh meat and biscuits. This routine, or something very similar would happen every day whilst he was a police dog, and for the rest of his life, and he liked it. He liked the attention and he loved the feel of the brushes going over his thick fur coat. An hour later he was back in the police dog van and on the way to the vet.

Constable Wood parked the police van in the car park at the side of the vet's surgery and he got Mr Ted out of the back and put him onto his lead.

"Don't look so worried Mr Ted, the vet here is very nice, you'll like him." he said as he led him into the surgery. He told the receptionist that he was there with Mr Ted for a check up, and once that was done they walked through into the waiting room. Mr Ted was sniffing at the floor showing a great interest in all the new scents that he found there. In the waiting room Mr Ted was surprised to see more animals. There was a Cocker Spaniel, two cats in separate cages, a Greyhound and a Jack Russell, all there with their anxious owners. The Cocker Spaniel was wagging his tail so fast that it was acting like a cooling fan to those around him. The greyhound's tail was between his back legs and not moving at all, he gave the impression to Mr Ted that he was not at all happy. The Jack Russell had a little stump of a tail and you couldn't tell if he was wagging his tail or if his whole body was shaking. But they all looked happy enough, except the greyhound, if their eyes were anything to go by. The dogs were all straining against their leads to get a closer look at Mr Ted, and the cats shrunk towards the back of their cages to get as far away from Mr Ted as they could. Mr Ted was very interested in the animals too, and he pulled towards the other dogs to get close to them. Constable Wood pulled him back and said, "Steady Ted." He'd never been to a vet's surgery before, not that he could remember anyway, it was all new to him and he wondered what everyone was doing there. He even wondered what he was doing there.

Mr Davidson had been the police vet for many years, and was well experienced in examining and treating police dogs. He had seen many before Mr Ted, just like him when they were starting out, and later when they became ill or injured, or just in need of routine top up injections once a year. After waiting for a while to take their turn to see the vet the receptionist said, "You can go through now Mr Wood."

He took Mr Ted along a short corridor and though a door into the vet's examination room. Inside Mr Ted could see the vet, he was standing behind a high counter and he was wearing a long white coat. He came around the high counter to stand in front of Mr Ted and spoke to him softly.

"Hello Mr Ted. I've been expecting you. You are a handsome boy, and you're going to be a police dog. How exciting is that?"

Mr Ted began to feel much more comfortable in the presence of the vet after that. He spent at least half an hour examining Mr Ted. He listened to his heart and lungs through a stethoscope, looked in his eyes and ears, examined his feet, weighed and measured him, and took a series of x-rays.

At the end of it all he declared, "Mr Ted, I am pleased to say that you are A1 fit for duty as a police dog, and good luck in your training."

Both Mr Ted and Constable Wood were pleased to receive this good news. Before they left the surgery Mr Davidson gave Ted a series of injections to protect him against common dog illnesses. None of this seemed to bother Mr Ted who was enjoying all the attention. Once all that was done Constable Wood said goodbye to Mr Davidson and took Mr Ted back to the police van and off they went, back to the kennels.

Constable Wood broke the good news to Sergeant Fleming who wasted no time in making the arrangements with the dog training school at Gapford, where Mr Ted was booked on the next available course.

Chapter Four

Training to be a Police Dog

Winter was setting in and the three month training course was going to last all through the winter into spring time. Much of the training would be done out in the open, both in the day time and at night, and hopefully by the spring Mr Ted would be a trained police dog. Police Constable Eddie Wood got Mr Ted up bright and early that first Monday morning, took him for a long walk in the park as usual and gave him his breakfast of meat and biscuits when they got back. He gave him a good combing which Mr Ted enjoyed as always. Then he put him into the Ford Escort Police van to drive him from the kennels at Wavehill to Gapford, a journey of seventy miles. Mr Ted had been in the same police van before and he felt quite at home there, in fact he got very possessive about it sometimes and instinctively barked if anyone dared to come too near to it. The van was sign written on the back doors with the words "CAUTION – POLICE DOGS IN TRANSIT". The side doors of the van had a Police crest on them and the word "POLICE" was painted across the bonnet. To cap it all off there was a large blue light on the roof and sirens hidden behind the radiator grille. Inside the van there was a special compartment behind the passenger seats for the police dogs, it was a secure caged area that the dogs could be kept safe and comfortable in.

Two hours later they were booking in at the dog training school reception where they were met by the sergeant trainer, Stan Austin. Both Mr Ted and Constable Wood were very apprehensive about this place. It was all very new to them, and they wondered what lay ahead. Sergeant Austin had been a police dog handler and trainer for years and years, and what he didn't know about dog training wasn't worth knowing. There were other people there too; two kennel maids who looked after the dogs, the Inspector in charge of the school, some more trainers and seven more new dogs and their handlers from police forces all over the country. Mr Ted and Police Constable Eddie Wood were to get to know these dogs and policemen over the next three months very well as they all went through their training under the watchful eye and skilled tuition of Sergeant Austin.

Mr Ted and Constable Wood were shown, by the kennel staff, to his new home for the three months that he would be there. It was a kennel block just like the one at Wavehill. Each of the new dogs was given a kennel and their name was written on a board outside it together with their handler's name. They would live in it until the end of the course. Mr Ted, although always cautious about any new surroundings, soon settled in and barked with the other dogs until they all had their say. Then they stayed quiet for the next couple of hours whilst Constable Wood and the others received their briefing from Stan Austin.

"I don't know what you lot have been told, or what you expect to find at the training school," said Sergeant Austin, "but you must remember that what I say goes while you're here. If you listen and learn then you won't go far wrong."

At the end of his first training talk he said, "Go and get your dogs on their leads and we'll do some obedience training on the sports field to start you off and to see how good these dogs are."

Constable Wood collected Mr Ted, put him on the lead and walked with all the others at a brisk pace down the track from the kennels through a very small wood and down a hill onto a flat rugby field. Mr Ted looking all around him as they walked along, taking in the scent and sounds of the wooded area he found himself in.

Stan Austin asked all eight handlers to stand in a line with their dogs on their left side and watch. Stan had got his own dog with him, a trained police dog called Sabre. Stan had Sabre on the lead on his left side, he said to the dog, "Sabre, heel!" and marched off like a soldier on parade, at a brisk pace, with Sabre marching alongside him. The dog was looking ahead, but looking up at the sergeant too, waiting for the next command. After a while the pair first turned right, then left, then completely about. They didn't put a foot wrong, and they were in perfect harmony with one another. As perfect a display of obedience as you would see anywhere including the Crufts dog show. "Sabre, halt!" came the command and the sergeant and dog stopped dead in their tracks. Mr Ted and Constable Wood looked on in admiration. "You are going to do that now." said Stan, "You first Wood."

Police Constable Wood tightened his hold on the lead and said "Mr Ted, heel!" and started to walk off. Mr Ted looked puzzled and didn't know what was expected of him, he looked up at Constable Wood for further direction and he only moved when the lead got tight as Constable Wood moved off a couple of paces, even then he was running around the front and back of Constable Wood, barking and jumping around. Nothing like the pristine display he had just observed, and the others that followed didn't do much better either. Both Constable Wood and Mr Ted felt awkward about their display, and hoped that things would get better. Mr Ted and Constable Wood would do this routine of marching up and down, and changing direction, every day for the duration of the course, and they would get better and better as each day passed. Eventually, every time he started off Mr Ted would be standing beside his master, and every time he was told to halt he would stop and stand alongside him too. As they got better at it they both felt better about the whole thing.

Next the sergeant showed them how the dogs would come back to the handler when they were called. This was done by Constable Wood having Mr Ted on the lead and running backwards with Mr Ted facing him and following to the command: "Mr Ted, come!" This routine was practised every day as well, and every day they would get better at it and the distance between the dog and handler would increase as far as the long training lead would allow. Coming back when you were called was just about the most important command a dog could learn and underpinned every other type of training that was to follow. To start with Mr Ted didn't understand what he was supposed to do, but with a little encouragement from Constable Wood and a light pull on the lead he soon got the idea. When Mr Ted started to get it right, Constable Wood praised him. This made Mr Ted feel good about what he was learning, and he began to enjoy it, and usually showed he was enjoying it by wagging his tail.

At the end of the first day, and they didn't do any more than practise heel walking and coming back, Stan decided that he would test what they had all learnt and said to the handlers, "Right lads, let your dogs off the lead, start walking, give the command "heel" and march them back to the kennels." Full of confidence at the training they had been given, Constable Wood let his dog off the lead, and all the other handlers did the same with their dogs.

Before anyone could say "Heel" all the dogs, delighted to be set free, and thinking that the training was over, ran off around the field barking and chasing each other. Every handler shouted their dog's name and the command "Come!" None of the dogs took the slightest bit of notice. The sergeant laughed to himself knowingly and walked off, with his police dog Sabre off the lead firmly at his side, back to the kennels for tea. As he looked back he could see all the handlers chasing their dogs and shouting at them, and the dogs enjoying the game! They did get rounded up, eventually, and back at the kennels Mr Ted was fed and settled down for the night, feeling quite content with life.

The next morning by eight o'clock Mr Ted was woken up by the sound and scent of Police Constable Wood and the others approaching the kennel block. He loved it when he could hear Constable Wood coming to get him; he knew it meant that they would be together. He was treated to a good brushing; making his beautiful black and tan coat shine with the care and attention it got from Constable Wood. Then off they went back to the dog training area next to the rugby field at the other side of the woods and down the hill from the kennels. As they made their way through the wood they passed a whelping block. It looked much like the main kennel block; brick built with windows, electric light and heat, but used specifically for breeding mothers to have their puppies in comfort and style. The sergeant asked them all to be as quiet as possible and to look through the window, where inside they could see a German Shepherd bitch tending to six tiny German Shepherd puppies. "They were all born last night," said Stan Austin. "They are all going to be police dogs and they are known as the *B* litter. All of them will have names beginning with the letter *B*. See that black one there? We've already named him *Mount Browne Blue Strobe*, but he'll be known as Blue. They will all be in here for a few weeks cared for by their mother and the kennel staff." Mr Ted, curious about what was inside the kennel, jumped up at the window of the whelping block and he could see the pups inside too, before Constable Wood told him to get down again.

When they arrived at the training field they repeated the exercises from the day before once more, as they would do every day. After a while Stan asked them all to join him at a series of wooden jumps. Some high, some low, and others quite long. Stan explained that the dogs were all going to learn to jump cleanly over these obstacles, and it was an essential part of their training, just as important as obedience training. When they were operational police dogs they would need to be able to scale and jump obstacles, and this was how they learnt to do it. Like the obedience they all started off not knowing what or how to do it, but after being shown by Sergeant Austin and Sabre they all practised at it until they started to get it right, and like everything else they would practise this every day. Mr Ted didn't think much of this new game at first, but when he jumped over one of the jumps and Constable Wood showered him with praise, he began to enjoy it. The more praise he got the better he performed and the better he liked it.

After lunch they were introduced to searching for things that were hidden from view. Their favourite ball or toy was used at first, and the dogs were asked to go and look for it. After watching their handlers go behind a tree or building to put it down, the dogs ran forward on the lead with the handler until they found it. Constable Wood was told to use the command "Seek" when Mr Ted's turn came. Mr Ted's favourite toy was a tennis ball. He watched excitedly as Constable Wood went off with it in his hand to hide it, and he couldn't wait to get after it and find it for himself. Mr Ted thoroughly enjoyed this new game and was very keen to have a go at it as often as he could.

Sergeant Austin said, "Mr Ted has got the making of a good search dog, he really likes this and he's got a keen nose for it."

Mr Ted seemed to understand the praise, especially when PC Wood patted him fondly and with some pride in his dog's ability.

"Well done Ted. I'm proud of you."

Once again this exercise was practised every day, and the dogs would get better and better at it. Eventually learning that "Seek" meant they had to look for any hidden object or hidden person, whether it was in a building or out in the open somewhere.

Last thing that day they were all taught about tracking. This is where police dogs use their noses again, just like searching for things that are hidden, only this time they were scenting the ground to follow a trail left by a person. To make it easy for the first time that Mr Ted did it, Stan Austin held on to Mr Ted's lead and told Constable Wood to walk off towards the pavilion, then walk behind it out of sight and once out of sight to go into the wooded area behind the pavilion and hide. Mr Ted was straining at his lead, wanting to get after Constable Wood and to find out where he was going. Once Constable Wood had been gone a few minutes, Sergeant Austin let Mr Ted off his lead. Mr Ted ran off as fast as he could to where he last saw Constable Wood. Then he was lost, completely lost, until that is he put his nose to the ground and smelt the scent of Constable Wood's footprints on the ground. A human usually can't see where someone has walked, but Mr Ted could smell the difference in the ground where Constable Wood had walked compared to the ground around the scent, and Mr Ted had found the scent and he knew it. He knew he was on the trail of his handler. His sense of smell is many times greater than any human, and it was this sense of smell that would help Mr Ted through his training and make him a successful police tracking and search dog. Mr Ted followed the scent trail around the side of the pavilion to the back of the building, then in a straight line to the woods. He then went into the woods for about ten metres where he found Constable Wood lying down behind a tree trunk. Mr Ted barked with excitement at what he had found and Constable Wood made a great fuss of him; Mr Ted knew he had done well, especially when Sergeant Austin came running up to them.

"I told you that dog has got a good nose. There'll be no trouble training him to be a good tracking dog."

Mr Ted was encouraged to bark every time he found someone hiding, he liked barking, so that suited him fine. Mr Ted eventually learnt to bark on command when Constable Wood said, "Mr Ted. Speak!" He soon got the hang of that, and didn't take too much encouragement to bark on most occasions!

The tracking of people over long distances was practised in daytime and night time over a variety of terrain. After that first exercise Mr Ted did all his tracking by wearing a tracking harness around his body, and instead of a lead the harness was attached to a rope that extended to ten metres or so. This allowed him the freedom to use his nose to stay on the scent, and also allowed him to move from side to side and in circles unrestricted if the scent got difficult to follow until, that is, he could pick it up again. Constable Wood could tell when Mr Ted was following a scent because he pulled so hard on his harness, and his tail moved fast.

Over the course of the next few weeks the dogs and handlers practised these training exercises at as many different locations as they could find. Not always at the dog training school, but out in the woods and commons of Southdown, alongside rivers and roads, on industrial estates and in the grounds of large houses, and sometimes inside the large houses and factories of Southdown. All this was done to get the dogs used to working inside buildings and used to passing traffic and people. Progressively, they got better at each exercise until it became second nature. They became so good that they could do all that they had been taught off the training lead, obeying their handler's every command, just like Sabre, the sergeant's dog, on the first day. Mr Ted enjoyed the work and the variety. He looked forward to every new day of training. Being shown new things and new places every day made him a happy dog.

Around about week four of the course, once all the obedience training and agility training was at a high enough standard, and the sergeant was sure that the dogs were obedient; they were introduced to a series of exercises that would involve them being taught to seek out, and catch criminals. If a police dog couldn't do this kind of work he just couldn't be a police dog. He had to be good at everything, fearless in the face of aggression and always obedient to his handler's commands. They started this training by

Sergeant Austin shouting at Mr Ted whilst he was on the lead and once Mr Ted started barking at him the Sergeant ran away from him. Constable Wood followed him with Mr Ted on the lead shouting for the Sergeant to stop. When he did stop Mr Ted was encouraged to bark at him and run around him to keep him still. Once he had done that enough times and he was praised every time, Mr Ted soon picked up what he was supposed to do, and he liked the chasing and barking.

Later on, the chasing and cornering of criminals went a stage further when the Sergeant, acting the part of the criminal, used a stick or a knife in his hand, and later a gun. On these occasions Mr Ted was taught to attack the arm holding the weapon and force it from the "criminal" by biting hard on his hand or arm. He did this so well and with such enthusiasm that the sergeant spoke to Mr Ted about it.

"You've got courage Mr Ted, lots of it."

Mr Ted and Constable Wood were pleased to hear that, it meant they were doing well. These exercises, like all the rest, were done in the daytime and at night, inside and outside buildings and in all sorts of different places. As part of his training to make sure

Mr Ted was as brave and as strong as he looked one particular test of courage and aggression was done in a dark and unusual place where there was no light, fast flowing water, and lots of strange noises. Constable Wood and Mr Ted both knew that a special test was going to happen, but they didn't know what it was going to be. They would soon find out.

One night Mr Ted and all the other dogs being trained were taken with their handlers to a large country house which was surrounded by its own farmland, many acres of it including some woods, fields and farm buildings. Outside the house, about fifty metres in front of it, was a large man-made lake. Right in the middle of the lake was a fountain. The lake was fed with water from a river that ran through the estate into it. It was how this water was drained that was to be Mr Ted's biggest test of courage, although he didn't know that when they jumped out of the police van together.

It was around midnight, very dark with no light from the moon. It was raining and a strong wind was blowing the rain sideways into Mr Ted and Constable Wood. They braced themselves against the cold wind and the rain as Mr Ted looked all around him. Scenting the air, and wondering what was coming next. So was Constable Wood as they were given their instructions by Sergeant Austin.

"You are to take Mr Ted and walk around the side of the lake until you find a concrete ramp leading downhill alongside it. You are not allowed to take a torch or anything to light the way. I want you to operate in complete darkness just you and your dog. At the bottom of the ramp you will see an entrance to a dark tunnel. You must let Mr Ted off the lead and search the tunnel until you can get no further into it. If you find anything you are to do what the training you've had and what your instincts tell you. Mr Ted will help you with this one. There is water running out of the tunnel so be careful. Do you understand what you have to do?"

"Yes sergeant" said Constable Wood, seriously wondering what challenge lay ahead for him and Mr Ted.

They set off alone down the concrete ramp until they reached the bottom.

"What can all this be about Mr Ted? It's all a bit spooky." Mr Ted looked up at Constable Wood as if to say, "I don't mind what it is. I just like being out working."

It was so dark that they both had trouble seeing the entrance to the tunnel at first. When they did make it out in the gloom they could hear fast running water coming out of it towards them. The concrete path that they had been following led them straight to the entrance and into the path of the water. Constable Wood leant down and took Mr Ted's lead off him and told him to wait. They stood, listened and looked into the darkness of the tunnel. Looking was no good; it was as black as a witch's hat inside there. Listening was a bit better, but only because they could hear a couple of things, one was the sound of fast flowing water over the concrete river bed. The other noises though were the weirdest noises they had ever heard, coming out of the darkness was the sound of something banging. It was something like a heavy metal door slamming or something crashing onto metal, or metal hitting metal. They hadn't got a clue what it was, and that noise was accompanied by the sound of a roaring noise. It was a muffled roaring noise and could have been anything thought Constable Wood to himself. He couldn't make out if it was human, animal or something else. The darkness, the wet and the cold were beginning to get to him and make his mind think the unthinkable. How deep

48

was the water? Where did the tunnel lead? What would they find if they dared to get to the end? None of these questions had any answers. Who knows what Mr Ted was thinking, but he didn't seem to mind any of it. He looked keen to get on with it.

Mr Ted was off the lead, just as the Sergeant had ordered, but Constable Wood probably would have preferred to keep him on it in this strange and dark place. Taking a deep breath he gave Mr Ted the command "Seek." Mr Ted set off in front of him into the darkness and the water.

As they walked forward he couldn't see Mr Ted at all, but he could hear him splashing slowly through the cold running water, and he could hear him breathing. He would not be able to see if Mr Ted found anything. He would have to rely on sound alone for that. As they walked forward the water got up to his knees and up to Mr Ted's body. Nevertheless, Mr Ted kept going forward and was always a step or two ahead of Constable Wood. The water was flowing fast and strong around them, and the floor, although solid, was very slippery and slimy under foot.

He was worried that the water would get deeper, or there might be holes in the floor that would make him and Mr Ted trip up or fall into deeper water. They moved slowly and gingerly forward, taking what seemed like an age to make any forward progress at all into the darkness. Constable Wood kept close to the side of the tunnel, using his hand to help him feel his way. The sounds got louder the deeper they went into the tunnel. They turned one bend and then another, still in total darkness. Above all the other noises, which were still going on, and just as they passed the second bend there came the deafening noise of an explosion, which echoed around the tunnel walls and ceiling. It made Constable Wood and Mr Ted stop where they were. Both of them couldn't work out what the explosion was. When that noise had subsided, the other banging and roaring noises carried on as before. Mr Ted let out a bark as he heard the bang, and they could both feel the shock of the explosion.

They started to move forward again. Along the way PC Wood slipped on the slippery surface under the water and lost his footing for a moment, but got it back by falling against the tunnel wall. Even Mr Ted was slipping as he walked along and he had four feet on the ground!

The noises by now were much louder, the banging was still there but it was irregular and there was still no way of telling what it was, and now Constable Wood thought he could hear another sound. He made Mr Ted stop, and they both stood in the darkness and listened, mixed up in the roaring and banging was the sound of what he thought was screaming and shouting. He wondered if it was his mind playing tricks with him, or could he really hear someone shouting.

They had been in the tunnel for fifteen or twenty minutes he figured, all the time listening to the noises and moving slowly forward to avoid slipping or falling in the dark. It crossed his mind to give up and leave the tunnel and the noises and go back outside, but that would mean certain failure, they had to go on. Then there was another one of those horrifying explosions, just like before, the sound echoing all around them. After a few more metres they turned yet another corner and Constable Wood thought he could see a faint light in the distance. He dismissed it as his eyes playing tricks on him at first, but no, as they moved slowly forward it was getting stronger. He could just begin to make out the shape of Mr

Ted now, only the shape of him in the darkness and not much more. Mr Ted could see Constable Wood too.

As they crept forward they came to yet another bend in the river tunnel, followed by another, all the time the light getting brighter and the noises getting louder. Mr Ted's courage never faltered; he kept going forward ahead of Constable Wood. When they turned the last bend they could see ahead of them, about twenty metres away, water falling from above the tunnel like a waterfall, the fall of the water was making a loud roaring noise as it hit the ground below and flowed towards them. Behind the waterfall the dark shape of something that looked like a giant brown bear stood up on its hind legs, screaming and banging a heavy chain against a metal ladder! The ladder led from the floor up through the waterfall to the ceiling. Behind that image was a bright electric arc light that lit up the whole area and the bear like silhouette. The noise was deafening and the image terrifying.

Mr Ted ran forward once he could see the silhouette in the water. To him, in amongst all the noise, light and shadows it looked like a man shouting at him and Constable Wood. Mr Ted sensed danger. His barking echoed around the tunnel and added to the already deafening noise. Then there was another loud explosion. It came from something the shape was carrying. At the same time as the explosion there was a flash of flame coming out of it. Constable Wood shouted at Mr Ted to keep quiet and when he stopped barking he shouted at the bear shaped figure to come out of the water that was falling all over him from above. The shape stepped forward and through the falling water. As it did so he could see that it was a man dressed in heavy waterproof clothing and carrying a chain and a shotgun. The man fired the shotgun once more sending a deafening noise all around them and a bright flash coming out of the end of the gun.

"Attack Ted! Attack!"

Mr Ted knew they were under attack, and that he had to act quickly. He knew what he had to do. He was already on his way and had launched himself off the ground at full speed onto the dark figure, grabbing the arm that was holding the gun in his jaws.

"Drop the gun, now!"

The man did as he was told at once, shouting for the dog to let go of his arm. Constable Wood called Mr Ted and he let go at once, but never stopped looking at and barking at the man. Before

53

Constable Wood could do any more Sergeant Austin uncovered his face and switched on his torch so that they could see who he was.

"He did well in all that dark and all that noise. We knew that Ted was brave already, but that test shows that he is very courageous."

Once Mr Ted could see that it was Sergeant Austin he stopped barking and wagged his tail. He knew that he had done well and they could all leave the tunnel with a job well done.

That was the end of their training for that night. The next day and every day after that the practising went on, until every exercise was as good as the dog and handler could get it. It was very important to get it all right because in the last week of the course there was to be a test of all the exercises. Marks would be awarded according to the guidance in the Manual of Police Dog Training. Every dog and handler had to pass the test before they could get a certificate from the school that authorised them to work back in their home counties. The test for Mr Ted's course was at the start of the last week and would be judged by an experienced dog section Inspector from the Metropolitan Police.

Constable Wood and Mr Ted were both looking forward to the test, but at the same time they were a bit nervous because they wanted to do well and certainly didn't want to fail.

On the Tuesday of the test week Constable Eddie Wood got Mr Ted up early as usual, groomed him until his coat shone like a mink. He put a new collar on Mr Ted and went off for a last minute rehearsal, in obedience and agility, before the test.

"Mr Ted I think you have worked really hard on this course, and you and I know you can do well. We can both do this, we just need to work hard and show them what we can do. Do you agree?" Mr Ted looked at Constable Wood and barked.

"Let's go then shall we?"

It was Mr Ted's and Constable Wood's turn to take the test at 11 o'clock. They started off with the obedience test, marching up and down together, turning about and stopping when told to do so. Next the commands to sit then stand and bark came. All off the lead, and all of this so far performed by Mr Ted as if he was born to it. They moved on to searching for things hidden in the wood by Sergeant Austin, and then tracking by following a scent that the Sergeant had laid down in the grass sports field two hours before.

Mr Ted did all that was asked of him. Next came the test of courage and Mr Ted had to face a man holding a stick, then a gun. He got the gun and the stick from the man's hand with no trouble at all. Finally, a test of chasing after a running criminal and stopping him by circling and barking, and finding an injured person in the woods by using his nose to find him and barking loudly to let Constable Wood know what he had found.

Mr Ted enjoyed it all. He liked working and he loved the life at the training school where he could work all day every day. He loved to please Constable Wood by doing well, and he especially loved the praise that Constable Wood gave him every day, and this test day was just like any other training day for Mr Ted. It was a day to please and a day to enjoy.

Marks were awarded for each part of the test and they were diligently written down on the form with Mr Ted's name on it by the Metropolitan Police Inspector. All the other dogs and handlers were put through their paces too, and marked according to how well they had done. At the end of the day all the dogs and handlers were gathered together outside the pavilion on the sports field. Sergeant Austin and the Inspector had been comparing notes and writing on the test reports, and then they called the group to order and asked them to listen to the Inspector.

"I have enjoyed my time here today and I can say, without fear of contradiction, that the standard I have seen is outstanding. You are a credit to your forces, each other and the training school. Well done to you all. Every one of you has passed. Congratulations."

Everyone was delighted, the handlers threw their hats into the air, the dogs all barked and they were all let off the leads to run around. The difference this time was when Constable Wood called Mr Ted to heel, he obeyed at once with a wagging tail and happy bark, not like that first day of training when all the dogs, Mr Ted included, disobeyed the handlers and ran uncontrollably all over the field.

At the end of the week there was a passing out ceremony, where the dogs and handlers were on parade before the Chief Constable of Southdown. In turn they were all presented to the Chief who awarded them with a certificate. At the end the Chief Constable congratulated them all.

"I want to present a special award to the dog and handler team that has excelled above all others on this course in every discipline of dog training; whether its agility, searching and tracking or courage and I am pleased to say that the award goes to Mr Ted and Constable Wood."

Constable Wood and Mr Ted stepped forward and a rosette was clipped to Mr Ted's collar and Constable Wood was presented with a shield with their names on it, everyone clapped and both Mr Ted and Eddie Wood had great big smiles on their faces.

Sergeant Austin closed the proceedings by thanking the Chief Constable and wishing the dogs and their handlers good luck and good fortune as teams working together, and he said he hoped that they would have many adventures and put all that they had learned to good use protecting the public in the areas where they were going to work. Mr Ted and Constable Wood left the training school that Friday afternoon, sad to be leaving their friends and the school behind, but excited at the thought of going back home to work as a team together. Constable Wood drove them back to the Dog Section offices at Wavehill and reported to the Dog Section Sergeant. Sergeant Fleming looked at the certificate awarded to Mr

Ted and Constable Wood, congratulated them warmly and announced that they were to have the weekend off and then start their duties by reporting for the night shift the following Monday in Hawkridge.

Constable Wood took Mr Ted for a walk around the park. This time Mr Ted was allowed to go for his walk off the lead. Anyone could tell that Mr Ted enjoyed this walk in the park better than all those that he had been on before. He was free to walk at his own pace, but he never strayed very far from Constable Wood.

Chapter Five

The First Night on Patrol

That first night Constable Wood got Mr Ted ready for work. He was brushed until his coat shone as usual, and then he got into the back of the Ford Escort police dog van. Constable Wood made sure that he had got Mr Ted's lead and his training harness.

"Okay Mr Ted. This is it, off we go then."

Constable Wood got into the driver's seat, switched on the radio and called up the force headquarters control room.

"Alpha 41 and Police Dog Ted, we are on patrol in the Hawkridge area, over."

"Thank you Alpha 41."

The first hour or so went quietly enough with Mr Ted making himself comfortable in the back of the van. At one point he lay down and began to snore.

"Mr Ted, wake up! You're a trained police dog now, and you're on duty. No sleeping on duty."

The police radio burst into life, "Alpha 41, Alpha 41 are you receiving over?"

"Alpha 41, yes go ahead."

"Will you please go straightaway to St Michaels Social Club, Westbourne Road? The alarm is sounding there, and we believe there are intruders on premises."

Constable Wood understood the message, and made his way to the club house. It was just gone midnight and the club would have been locked up for the night over an hour ago, he thought to himself. There was every chance that there would be burglars on the premises, intent on stealing money, cigarettes and bottles of spirits. He also knew that because the alarm had gone off at the police headquarters, and he was told it was a silent alarm, he had up to twenty minutes to get there before the bells started ringing on the outside of the club. If he could get there before the bells started ringing then he and Mr Ted stood a better than good chance of catching the burglars in the act. He sped off in the van, talking to

Mr Ted all the way, encouraging him to be alert and ready for action.

"Right Mr Ted, we're off! There might be some burglars for us to catch. Let's see what we can do shall we?"

The blue light was going around on top of the van and he and Mr Ted could hear the noise of the motor making the blue bulb go around. Mr Ted could tell by the urgency in Constable Wood's voice that they were off to do some police work together. Mr Ted began to get excited in the back of the van, turning around and around in his space and barking excitedly at the prospect of going into action.

As they drew into Westbourne Road Constable Wood switched off his blue light and headlights and glided slowly up to the club entrance where he parked the van. He got Mr Ted out of the back and put him on his lead.

"Come on Ted; let's see if all that training has done you and me any good."

They walked around the outside of the building. It was very dark; there was not much light coming through the clouds in the sky, and only a very small amount of moonlight getting through every now and then as the clouds passed overhead in the breeze. Constable Wood discovered an open door to the fire exit at the side of the building. It should have been locked tight, but it was open, and he could see that the door had been forced open. It was clear to him now that the club had been broken in to.

He had no way of knowing if anyone was still inside or if they had fled. He knew what to do next, their training had prepared them for this moment, and he needed Mr Ted. He took him off his lead and made him sit beside him while he shouted through the open door.

"Police! Come out now or I will send in the dog!"

There was no response at all from inside the dark club. Constable Wood sent Mr Ted in.

"Find them Ted!"

Mr Ted, keen to get working, rushed into the darkness inside the building. Eddie Wood could hear him running inside the room, the noise of his paws on the tiled floor were clear and distinctive. There was no other sound coming from inside as Mr Ted swooped from one side of the large bar area to the other, using all his senses to work out where he was and if anyone was there. Then suddenly

Ted gave out a loud bark. Constable Wood heard screams and voices shouting.

"Help! Get the dog away from us! We give up."

"Good boy Ted! Keep them there!"

He ran inside the dark room and into the direction that he heard the voices; he shone his police torch towards the shouts and saw three young men standing beside the club's games machines. On the floor beside them was a torch, a screwdriver and a bag of money that they had stolen from the machines.

"Please Mister, get the dog away, he's frightening me."

"Down Mr Ted!"

Ted dropped to the floor, barking all the time at the burglars.

"You lot are under arrest for burglary. Stay exactly where you are and keep still if you know what's good for you."

This threat made the burglars even more nervous and they did exactly as they were told. The police radio that Constable Wood was carrying crackled into life.

"Alpha 41, can we have an update?"

"We have three men in custody for burglary, please send the prisoner van. There is stolen property to pick up as well."

The van soon arrived and when it did the three prisoners were taken quietly to it escorted by a watchful Mr Ted until they were safely locked inside.

The manager of the club was called by the police control room, and he was able to lock the club up again, after which he thanked Constable Wood and Mr Ted for their work, shook Constable Wood by the hand and patted Mr Ted on his head. Praise indeed for a good night's work well done. Dog and handler went back to their van and continued with their patrol of the streets of Hawkridge. Constable Wood was as proud as any police dog handler could be. He was proud of the fact that Mr Ted had performed just like an experienced police dog, doing exactly the right things in the club by finding and catching the burglars until Constable Wood could get inside to arrest them.

"You are a good boy Ted, you just carry on like that and you'll be the best police dog in the force."

Mr Ted barked and wagged his tail. He was pleased with himself.

The rest of the night passed quietly enough with Constable Wood driving around on patrol, and Mr Ted either lying down in the back of the van or standing up behind Constable Wood, looking through the cage and over his shoulder out to the road ahead. Then, about 3 o'clock, over the police radio another call for the services of Mr Ted came.

"Please go to Langford Road, Hawkridge. We have reports of a Ford car being driven erratically around the shops in the area."

"We're on our way."

They were only a mile away and with no traffic about at that time of night were able to get there quickly. As Constable Wood drove the police van in to Langford Road, just by chance, they passed a Ford car coming in the opposite direction; very fast. The driver was driving far too fast for the speed limit, and certainly too fast for the road conditions, there was no one else in the car. Constable Wood guessed that it might be the car that the force control room had sent them to investigate and turned the police van around in the street to go after it. He had no sooner turned around than he saw the Ford pick up speed and drive away from them. It was obvious that the Ford driver was trying to get away as fast as he could. Constable Wood put on the blue flashing light on top of his van and sped off after the car. Mr Ted sensed that something was happening and began turning around and around in the back of the van, barking as loud as he could, desperate to get involved in the chase himself.

"We are chasing a Ford saloon in Eaton Road towards the airport. I'm going to try and stop him."

"All right, keep us updated, over."

Constable Wood got close up behind the car and flashed his headlights signalling for the driver to pull over. He didn't, and sped off again. Constable Wood accelerated more and overtook the speeding car and put on the "POLICE – STOP" sign at the back of his van. The car driver ignored it and overtook the police van, looking at Constable Wood as he sped past. Constable Wood got a good look at the driver's face, and thought that he knew him. He recognised him as a young car thief, who had been in trouble with the police before for stealing cars. He had a reputation for running away when he saw the police and not stopping his cars when he was asked to.

Constable Wood got passed him a couple more times, but still he refused to stop, and the chase went on and on around the streets of Hawkridge. Luckily it was the middle of the night and there were no other cars or people about. The driver got ahead of the police van one more time and raced his car towards the countryside, on the road from Hawkridge to Enmore in the next county, a wide dual carriageway road, and as it left the boundary of 7the town the speed limit was supposed to be forty miles an hour, but the Ford was doing at least eighty, getting faster and more daring as it sped away from the chasing police van.

Just as the road bends to the left, near the county boundary the fleeing car lost control. It spun around two or three times before ending up on the wrong side of the road, facing the wrong way, and crashed sideways on into a lamp post! The car came to a dead stop; the driver let himself out of the driver's door and ran off, looking over his right shoulder at the police van as it sped towards him. He ran into the fields at the side of the road and into the darkness away from the street lights. He kept on running desperate to escape. He was running for his freedom. He knew he was in trouble for stealing the car, and for driving away from the police when told to stop. Seconds later Mr Ted and Constable Wood were at the scene of the crash. They both saw him get out of the car and run into the darkness. Constable Wood pulled up alongside the crashed car, and as he was letting Mr Ted out of the back of the van he called into his police radio.

"He's crashed and we're in pursuit on foot."

Although Mr Ted knew what to do, and was keen to get on with the chase, Constable Wood made him stand by his side for a second and wait.

"Stop or I will release the dog!"

The running man ignored him, shouting something back at Constable Wood that he couldn't quite hear.

"Stop him Ted!"

Mr Ted took off after him. He had a hundred metres start on Mr Ted, but there is no way that any human can out run a police German Shepherd in full flight, especially one as fit and as strong as Mr Ted. A hundred metres was nothing to him. He caught up with him in a few seconds and didn't he know it? Mr Ted looked massive to him and very menacing in the dark, and he was menacing. Mr Ted meant to stop the runaway and, as he got right up to him, he could hear the thud of the dog's feet hitting the ground behind him. He could hear him breathing, then there was the most terrifying sound of all, Mr Ted barking! It was a loud ferocious bark that would frighten the strongest and most fearless.

He looked over his shoulder once more just in time to see Mr Ted running right there, alongside him. He was exhausted, and the last thing he needed right now was a fight with a big police dog; he knew he had no chance of winning. He stopped in his tracks and Mr Ted circled him, running around and around barking all the time, keeping him in one spot until Constable Wood caught up.

"Are you going to come quietly?"

"Yeah, sure." he said, and he meant it.

Constable Wood shouted to Mr Ted, "Down Ted!" and Mr Ted dropped to the ground lying there barking. Constable Wood walked up to him, took him by the arm and led him back to the police van, under arrest for stealing the car. Mr Ted watched carefully until he was in the back of the van. When Mr Ted got into the back of the van, on his side of the two compartments there, he carried on letting the prisoner know that he was there and watching him by barking all the way to the central police station. No one was ever going to get away from Mr Ted once he'd captured them.

When they got back to the police station Constable Wood handed over the prisoner to the duty sergeant, and once he was locked up safely for the rest of the night the sergeant asked if he could see Mr Ted. Constable Wood brought Mr Ted into the police station to meet Sergeant Earle.

"This place is filling up with prisoners that you've caught tonight Mr Ted, carry on like this and you'll make one of the best dog and handler teams that this force has seen in a very long time."

Mr Ted understood what the sergeant was saying all right. He knew when he was being praised, and to show that he understood, he wagged his tail and barked, just the once.

At the end of their night shift they went back to the dog kennels at Wavehill Police Station, where the pair went for a walk in the park. Mr Ted running around free, but all the time looking back at Constable Wood to make sure he was still nearby. Constable Wood was reflecting on a good night's work, and really pleased with Mr Ted and the part he played in catching the criminals. Back at the kennel Mr Ted had a plate of well deserved food for his breakfast, a bowl of water, and a clean bed to sleep in until the next night's work. Mr Ted was tired and sleepy.

This routine went on for a week. Some nights were busier than others, and the days were spent quietly resting in the kennels. The other dogs were getting to know Mr Ted and there were normally some of the other dogs and handlers out on patrol when Mr Ted was at home. There was always great excitement in the kennel block at shift change over time, all the dogs barking and hoping that it was their turn to go out on patrol in the police van.

After a week of night duty there followed a week of late afternoon and evening work, then a couple of days off, then a week of early shift followed again by a couple of days off. Mr Ted loved his time on duty in the van with Constable Wood. Sometimes, when there was not much in the way of catching criminals to do, Mr Ted and Constable Wood would arrange to meet up with another trained police dog and handler team to practise all the things that they had been taught at the dog training school in Southdown. Sometimes it was searching for things, sometimes obedience work and sometimes agility. All this kept Mr Ted fit, obedient and well trained, and guess what? He loved it.

Chapter Six

Two children have gone missing in very suspicious circumstances

Thomas and Edwin were aged four and six years. Edwin was the eldest of the two and they were great pals as well as brothers. They lived with their mum and dad, Mr and Mrs Stapleton at 56 Rubery Drive, in Hawkridge. Edwin and Thomas were just like any other boys, full of life, full of fun and sometimes a little mischievous. One afternoon in the summer after school they had been playing with each other and a near neighbour and friend, Michael who was Edwin's age, in the garden of their house. After a while they asked Mrs Stapleton if they could all go to Michael's garden to play.

"All right then, but Edwin you must look after Thomas. You're older than him and he needs you to look after him. I want you back here in an hour for your tea. I'll come and get you. Don't go near that pond or the wood."

Off the three boys went. They had done it many times before and they would be quite safe in Michael's garden, just as they were in their own, it was only three houses away after all. As soon as the three boys walked out of the Stapleton house garden gate they headed for Michael's house, but instead of going in as they should have done, they walked straight past the house, along the road to a field at the end of the road. There was no fence around the field; there was lots of short grass for children to play on, a small wood at one end with about fifty trees and lots of bushes and shrubs in it. The sort of place where children sometimes like to build dens and hang about for a while, a secret place that only they know about. Of course the three boys couldn't let a visit to the field and the wood pass by without trying to climb a tree and hide in the bushes, which they did for a while, any thought of their mother's warning to stay away from the woods was gone from their memory. They were having fun. Beyond the wood was a large pond, just right for throwing stones into and a magnet for children of all ages.

Years before a young child had very nearly drowned in that pond, not that Edwin, Thomas and Michael knew anything about that. They did know though that their Mums didn't want them ever to go anywhere near the pond, and that it was wrong to go there or in the woods without their mums, but they thought that a quick visit wouldn't hurt, and they were having such fun throwing stones in the water and running around the edge of the pond. It was a beautiful warm sunny day, and they didn't know how long they had been there, but it didn't seem too long to them. They went back to their den in the wood, made from broken branches and fallen logs, when they heard someone else coming through the trees.

When they looked up they were startled and frightened when they saw a man. He was wearing a heavy long coat that went down past his knees, and he had a dirty black scruffy beard. His hair looked like a scarecrow's, long and matted. He looked frightening to them and he startled them even more when he started talking to them.

"Hello boys. Fancy you being here all alone. Where's your mum?"

He smiled at them in a sort of grin-like way, revealing dirty black teeth.

"Mum's at home." said Edwin, "We're just playing."

Michael didn't speak. He ran off back home. He was frightened by the strange man; he went straight to his house without turning around once, went indoors and said nothing to anyone about his time in the woods with the others.

It was long after an hour had passed that Mrs Stapleton went to Michael's house to collect her boys. She knocked on the door and Michael's mother answered it.

"Hello, I've come to collect the boys please. It's time for their tea."

She found out to her horror that Edwin and Thomas were not there and never had been. Michael's mother thought that he had been with Edwin and Thomas at their house. He was home now, but she didn't know where the other two were, she hadn't seen them at all.

"Have you seen Edwin and Thomas?" said his mum to Michael.

He didn't answer, and his mum said "Come on Michael. This is important, you look like you know something what is it?" Still Michael wouldn't answer.

Mrs Stapleton left Michael and his mother and ran out on to the street, she looked up and down and ran back to her own house. She searched every room, the garden, the garden shed and the garage; there was no sign of her two little boys. She searched it all again, but they were not there.

She ran back out into the street and was met by Michael's mother. "He's told me they went to the field and the wood, he said they were talking to a man and Michael ran away."

"How long ago?" said Mrs Stapleton,

"I don't know I can't get any more out of him."

Both of them ran to the wood, they looked in the field, in the wood and the pond. The boys had gone, and there was no sign of the man. Mrs Stapleton knocked on her neighbours' doors, rang some friends, she searched up and down the road a few more times as best she could. Time was ticking away and she was frantic with worry. Her little boys were missing and they were with a man in the woods when Michael left them. Her imagination was in overdrive and she feared for her children, she wanted them back, and she wanted them now, and above all she wanted them to be safe.

She went indoors and rang 999 to report the children as missing. She told the police as much as she knew and told them about the man in the woods. The first police car to arrive was driven by a policewoman. She talked to Mrs Stapleton and got as much of a description of the boys, in as much detail, as she could. She got details of their size, hair colour, and the clothes they were wearing and where they were last seen. She passed all this information, very quickly to the police control room and a description of the two missing little boys was passed out over the radio to every police patrol car and police officer on duty in the county that afternoon. The best guess that anyone could put on the time that they had been missing was two hours. A six year old and four year old could get into some serious trouble in that amount of time!

Four more policemen came to the house. They searched the house, the garden and the garage before moving on to the field and the wood. They searched that too, but found nothing. Then they started knocking on doors in the street, but no one knew where the boys were nor had they seen them. They had disappeared and no one, but no one, knew where they were. The police sergeant came from the police station to join the search. He got some neighbours together, and organised them into a search party. He asked them first to search all their gardens, sheds, garages and houses. That took another hour to do. When it was done he got them all together at the field. Here he asked them all, including the police officers, to walk side by side through the field, and side by side through the wood, looking for anything, anything at all that would give them a clue about the boys.

Six more police officers joined in the search, and a mobile police control van arrived in the street. The police sergeant decided to draw a circle on a map to show a search area. The first circle was a two hundred metre circumference around the boy's house. It took in the houses around it, the field, pond and the wood. The search team was tasked with searching in that area. Still there was no sign of the boys, and the search area was widened to double its size, to four hundred metres.

By 10 o'clock the boys had been missing for over five hours. It was dark now and a couple of hundred people, including the police officers, were searching inside the four hundred metre area. The boy's father had got home from work and he had been searching too. At quarter past ten, in the street beside the police control van, the night shift from the police station joined their colleagues who had been searching for the boys. Mr and Mrs Stapleton were in their house with a policewoman, going over the story again, and being kept informed of the progress being made in the search for Edwin and Thomas. Mrs Stapleton was crying uncontrollably thinking that her sons had been kidnapped and hoping and praying that no harm had come to them and that no one had hurt them.

Standing in the crowd of neighbours and police officers receiving instructions on where to look next and how to search was Mr Ted and Constable Eddie Wood. The Police Inspector was in charge of the briefing. There were press reporters, television cameras and radio reporters listening to him too.

"These two boys have been missing from their home for nearly six hours," said Inspector Griffiths. "We need to find them and we need to find them as quickly as we can. They will be hungry and frightened by now wherever they are. We mean to search all night and until we find them and get them back to their mother."

He told the volunteer searchers and the police that the search area would be widened to include the whole estate, and that he would like all the houses and gardens and garages searched as a priority. He split the people up into teams, each with a mix of police and volunteers.

"Our priority is to find the children, but while you are looking if anyone sees a man of scruffy appearance, with a beard, long hair and a long dark coat, keep hold of him and let me know straight away." said Inspector Griffiths.

"PC Wood I would like you and Mr Ted to have a search outside the area that the others are working in. Just see what you can turn up." said the Inspector.

Constable Wood went first to look at the field and wood where the boys were last seen. Mr Ted had a good look around, scenting the air as he went. Then they walked off up Rubery Drive together, determined to do what they could to find the boys. They went right to the edge of the housing estate and on to a big industrial estate. There were some factories and offices here, each with their car parks, and a series of roads running around and between the buildings. The street lights were on, but the buildings were all in darkness. There was no one about at all, except the two of them. Around the outside of the industrial estate was another wooded area. Constable Wood could see in places where the street lights shone, but there were plenty of dark places at the side of and behind the buildings. There was some light there though from the moon that was high overhead in the sky. Constable Wood let Mr Ted off his lead and told him to seek. Mr Ted, keen to get going, set about working between the buildings and the lorries and vans that were parked outside some of them. Constable Wood could see Mr Ted working with his nose to the ground, moving quickly, rushing from side to side in his search for fresh scent on the ground.

They must have gone around half of the estate when Mr Ted suddenly lifted his head up from the ground and ran over to a small white Vauxhall van that was parked in one of the car parks. The van looked abandoned to Constable Wood. Its lights were broken and the windows were open. Mr Ted was very interested in the van, running around and around it. Then he stopped and put his front paws onto the open window on the driver's side and put his head inside the van. He let out a quiet yelp.

"What have you got boy? What is it?"

Mr Ted got down and ran around the van twice more before putting his head in the driver's window again. Constable Wood looked inside the van himself, but couldn't see anything except a pile of old paper, clothing and tools. He opened the doors at the back of the van and Mr Ted jumped in. It was a bit like getting into the back of his police van, but much more untidy. There was nothing obvious in the van that Constable Wood could see, but Mr Ted was getting very excited and began pulling at an old coat that was lying there. Then, slowly as the coat was pulled away by Mr Ted, Constable Wood could see two small white faces. It was the faces of two little boys lying motionless on the floor of the van. Constable Wood called Mr Ted away; he didn't like what he saw. The boys looked like they had been placed there and covered up.

Back at the police control room the Inspector was getting reports from the search teams that said they had found nothing. Mr and Mrs Stapleton were there again now and she was crying and being held and supported by Mr Stapleton. Her boys had been missing for hours, it was past 11 o'clock and the boys should have been in bed, safe in their own home and fast asleep. Instead they were missing, no one could find them, and the last they knew was that they were seen talking to a strange man in the woods. A man that no one knew or could identify and, worse still, he was nowhere to be found either. The big question on everyone's mind was, did the man take the children away, and if he did what did he want with them? This is a thought that Mrs Stapleton couldn't bear to enter her head. She was frantic with worry and this story about the man made her worry a million times worse. She just wished the boys would come back.

The press were gathering in larger numbers now, and had been for a couple of hours. There was a story on Anglia News and Look East on the BBC, and it was on the local radio stations too. As well as this the national press had picked up the story of two missing children from Hawkridge and were arriving with their broadcast trucks and news reporters. They were all asking questions, filming the area as best they could in the dark, and wanting to know when they could interview Mrs Stapleton.

Arrangements were being made in the police control van to start letting some of the search teams go, and to get some other police officers to join the search. They had been searching for hours and found nothing. Some volunteered to stay on longer, and some police officers were going to stay and continue searching until the children were found or until they were relieved at six the following morning.

Constable Wood began to carefully pull away the coat covering the bodies of the two little boys in the van. Mr Ted was sitting on the ground outside but he could wait no longer, he knew he had been told to stay where he was but he decided to jump back into the van. He placed his cold wet nose onto the face of the eldest boy. Edwin opened his eyes and looked at the face of the German Shepherd and thought he was dreaming at first. As soon as Constable Wood saw that Edwin was alive and awake he said to him gently,

"I'm a policeman, and this is my police dog Mr Ted, we've been looking for you. Your mum will be pleased to see you my boy."

Constable Wood picked up Thomas, who was still fast asleep and put him over his shoulder, he took Edwin by the hand and walked them back towards their home. He had already radioed the police control van that he had found the boys alive and well. Mr and Mrs Stapleton, followed by a lot of other people, came running towards them.

Constable Wood handed the two boys over to their mum and she embraced them, relieved that they were alive. A cheer went up from the crowd that was around them, everyone happy that the boys were found and were safe back in the arms of their mother. As for Edwin and Thomas they were both rubbing their eyes, and wondering what all the fuss was about.

As soon as Constable Wood handed the children to Mrs Stapleton he and Mr Ted went the few yards back to the van. Mr Ted was getting agitated as they approached it. The closer they got the more agitated Mr Ted became. Constable Wood took Mr Ted off his lead, opened the back doors of the van.

"I'll tell you once, come out her now! Show yourself, or I'll put my police dog in there to get you out!"

There was no movement at all from inside the van.

"Get in there Ted. Find him!"

Mr Ted jumped into the back of the van and went straight for the wall at the front that separated the back of the van from the driver's seat. He leapt up onto a shelf above the driver's seat and started growling as he pulled at a sheet on the floor of the shelf.

"All right! All right! Get him away. I'll come out."

The scruffy bearded man sat up as he spoke. Constable Wood called Mr Ted out of the van.

"Well done Ted. Come here."

Constable Wood placed his handcuffs the man.

"You're under arrest for kidnapping. You didn't think that we were going to leave you in there did you? Mr Ted knew you were in there from the moment he first saw the van."

He led him back to the police control post where he was handed over to the sergeant. Mr Ted and Constable Wood knew that they had done well. The children were safe again, and even though they had been through a frightening experience they were back where they belonged. The scruffy man would go to jail for taking the two little boys. Thomas and Edwin never disobeyed their mother again.

Chapter Seven

Mr Ted meets a very important person

Mr Ted and Constable Eddie Wood followed a routine of police work. They always patrolled in the same police dog van with a variety of shifts around the twenty four hour clock. Sometimes it was early morning, sometimes late afternoon and sometimes night duty, with days off for rest in between. Every shift started with a good brushing of his coat by Eddie Wood. Mr Ted had learnt to stand with his front paws on a high step and his back paws on the floor. In this semi standing upright position Eddie would groom and brush Mr Ted just as they were taught at the police dog training school. First Eddie ran his hands over Mr Ted's furry coat, up and down, roughing it up and loosening up any unwanted hair and debris that might have got caught in it. Next came brushing with a firm brush, which again took away any loose hair, this was always followed by a soft brush to smooth Mr Ted's black and tan coat. It was finished off by running chamois leather over his fur. This final bit of grooming always made Mr Ted's coat shine really well. A well groomed dog is a happy dog, and whenever he was being groomed you could tell Mr Ted was happy. Not only did he wag his tail, a sure sign of happiness in any dog, but his eyes were bright, and he used to smile at Constable Wood, and sometimes let out a happy sounding bark of approval. Once all this was done Mr Ted got into his patrol van which had been cleaned ready for him, and off they would go on their daily duties. Constable Wood wearing his police uniform of black trousers, police jacket and flat cap.

One spring day in April Constable Wood and Mr Ted were asked by Sergeant Fleming, the dog sergeant, to join another police dog team to work on a special duty. The other team was Constable Brian Markham and police dog Della. Mr Ted and Della knew each other well; they had worked together before. They had also spent time in the kennels at Wavehill when they were not on patrol, looking through the bars that separated their exercise area and kept them apart. That didn't stop them taking a closer look at each other by putting their noses together through the bars, and barking at each other. They were both German Shepherds, both trained police dogs and shared exactly the same lifestyle. Better than that, they liked each other. The handlers and kennel staff sometimes took Mr Ted and Della out together on exercise walks in the nearby park, and they always got on well. It was obvious to everyone that Mr Ted and Della were the best of friends.

"What you have to do," said Sergeant Fleming, "is report for duty in your best uniforms, and with Mr Ted and Della brushed up smart with their best leads and collars on, at Broughton House mansion at 10 'clock on Wednesday night. You will be on night duty there all week after that. You will be met by Special Branch officers; they will be looking after some very important visitors to Broughton House and they will tell you what it is that you have to do there, and why they want police dogs to do it."

At a quarter to ten on Wednesday night two shiny white dog vans pulled into the gates of the grounds at the big house. They followed each other quietly as they turned off the main road that runs between Hawkridge and Enmore. Constable Wood and Mr Ted were in the lead van, followed by Della and Constable Markham. They drove slowly but purposefully along the private road that twisted and turned its way for about a mile, passing the gates to Home Farm on their right hand side. After another half a mile they could see the mansion with its light coloured sand stone walls standing out in the moonlight. There were lights on in a lot of the rooms, and there were a lot of rooms. The house was the home of Sir Harold Cosgrove and his family, cousin to Her Majesty Queen Elizabeth, the Queen of England. The grounds contained a lake, and a river ran through the whole estate from north to south. The property was protected by a high red brick wall with electric gates at the lodge houses, of which there were six. The gates were always kept closed, except the gate on the main road which was opened and closed to visitors to the estate by a security guard. The house itself was big, about as big as Buckingham Palace, the Queen's London home.

The two police dog vans pulled into the yard at the side of the house, where lots of other police cars and vans were parked. People were going to and from the vehicles unpacking them and carrying things into the house. It was obvious something big was about to happen. Once Constables Wood and Markham parked and got out of their vans they went over to the police control room. Inside they found Detective Inspector Lynch and Detective Sergeant Barnes and reported for duty to them. There were other teams of police officers there. They were all briefed on their duties for the coming few days and the purpose of it all. The Queen was coming to stay at Broughton House at the invitation of her cousin, and she was planning to stay for a few days. It was to be a private visit with no public engagements. Wherever the Queen goes she is protected by strict security, and this time Mr Ted would have a role to play in that. The dog handlers and the dogs were to patrol around the grounds all through the night, every night, whilst she was in residence. They would pay particular attention to the area around the mansion and make sure that no one disturbed Her Majesty.

Constable Wood agreed with Constable Markham that they would patrol mostly on foot and would split up, keeping in touch by police radio. On the first night they did just that, Constable Wood and Mr Ted walking in the woods and grassed areas around the house, checking the outside of the building making sure the doors and windows were secure, and the same checks were carried out on the cars that were parked outside. The only sounds that could be heard was the hoot of some nearby owls high up in the trees or in the barns of Home Farm, and sometimes the cry of a pheasant coming from the woods and fields. This was important work thought Constable Wood. He and Mr Ted were going to make sure that no one disturbed the Queen while they were there.

On the first night they were walking down one of the roads around the house at about 3 o'clock; Mr Ted was walking loose and off the lead when he saw something ahead of him. It startled him at first. He looked at Constable Wood to see what he thought of it, and then he looked back. It was the dark shape of a person standing still and facing him. To Mr Ted it looked like a very big man wearing a cloak and carrying something in his right hand. It could have been a stick or it could have been a shotgun. Whatever it was it was long and thin. Mr Ted stopped in his tracks and started to growl deeply, at the same time looking at Constable Wood for a reaction.

Mr Ted knew what to do; he just needed to be told to do it by Constable Wood. Mr Ted was ready to attack. To him the image he could see looked very menacing, he had no business being there and Mr Ted was going to do his duty and stop him before he could do any harm. He was growling deeper now, and the fur on the back of his neck was standing on end; a sure sign that he was not happy.

"What is it Ted?"

As soon as he heard Constable Wood speak Mr Ted began barking loudly at the dark figure and he ran towards it. The man didn't move at all, not a flicker of movement. As Mr Ted got closer still, barking and growling, still there was no movement.

The police radio burst into life, it was Constable Markham. "What's going on Alpha 41? I can hear Ted. What is it?"

"I'll let you know in a minute. Give me a minute, over."

Just as things were getting very tense and Mr Ted was about to attack the large man who stood there in silence, with the stick or gun under his arm, the moon came out from behind some clouds and lit up the scene. What Mr Ted and Constable Wood could see now was a six foot tall scarecrow! It was dressed just like a man, wearing a hat, trousers, coat and boots, and carrying a large stick in one of his straw hands. Mr Ted could see more clearly now what it was. He went right up to it and realised that there was no human scent, it was just a scarecrow.

"That was a bit spooky Mr Ted. It got you and me going for a minute." said Constable Wood as he used the radio to tell Constable Markham that it was nothing, and he would tell him later what the barking was all about. They carried on with their patrol all that night and all was quiet, no more scarecrows!

When it got light Detective Inspector Lynch called for Constable Wood and Mr Ted and gave them one more job to do before they could go off duty. In the garage at the back of the house was a car, a very special car. It was the Queen's Rolls Royce State Limousine. On top of its radiator grille was the unique silver mascot, always used by the Queen on her car, of St George slaying the dragon. On its roof was a heraldic shield bearing the Queen's coat of arms.

"I want you to search the garage, and search underneath the car and inside it to make sure that there is nothing in here that would cause Her Majesty any harm. Make sure that dog doesn't make the car dirty." The Inspector demanded.

Constable Wood and Mr Ted looked at the huge car. At first it looked black, a very shiny black, but when he looked closer Constable Wood could see that the car was actually a very dark Victoria plum colour, so dark in fact that it looked black. It shone like a mirror and Constable Wood could see himself and Mr Ted as if he was looking into a mirror. They set about working as a team searching first the garage on the inside and the outside, including the roof, then moved onto the car. Mr Ted sniffed all around the outside, and Constable Wood checked underneath. They both looked in the boot, the engine compartment and finally inside the car where the Queen sits. It was all clear, nothing was there and the car was safe to use. Before Constable Wood went to tell Inspector Lynch the good news, he found a clean cloth in the garage and used it to polish off the marks that Mr Ted had made on the shining bodywork of the car with his wet nose. Mr Ted looked on inquisitively.

The next night Constables Wood and Markham reported to Detective Inspector Lynch at 10 o'clock sharp. The briefing was the same as the night before. Once it was over the two dog handlers took their dogs, and as before split up on their patrols, promising to keep in touch with each other by radio. It was a fine night again, a little cool, with a light breeze and some cloud occasionally covering the moon. Constable Wood and Mr Ted spent the first couple of hours in the fields and gardens at the back of the mansion house and, apart from seeing a few rabbits and hearing owls in the trees, the time they spent on their patrol was not much more to them than an everyday walk, except they were always on the lookout for anything unusual. Later on they knew that they would be searching the garage and the car again, but for now it was outside patrol duty to make sure that no one but no one disturbed the Queen and the other guests in the house.

On the neatly cut lawn at the front of the house there were fifty or so rabbits running around and eating the grass. Mr Ted was used to rabbits; he had seen plenty of them on the farm before he joined the police. Then he used to have great fun chasing after them, never being able to catch them, but just chasing after them at top speed until they disappeared down a rabbit hole in the ground and out of reach. Now, after his police training he looked at them, he was very interested in them and he might have even wanted to chase after them, but he knew that his job was to stay with

Constable Wood and he did just that. He never let rabbits or any other animals distract him from what he was trained to do. His job was to work with Constable Wood and obey his every command, and he never told him to chase rabbits!

Around about midnight Mr Ted and Constable Wood were quite near the house in the garden when they saw the silhouette of a person walking in the dark against the back wall of the house. He or she was walking very slowly and looking about them from side to side as they went. Constable Wood whispered into his police radio, "Are you there PC Markham?"

"Yes, go ahead," he replied in a quiet whisper sensing that something was wrong.

"I can see someone at the back of the house near the French doors. I can't tell who it is or what they are doing. Watch the front."

"I'm there now." he replied over the radio.

"Watch him Ted. Watch him."

Mr Ted stood still and quiet, looking intently at the dark figure moving slowly at the back of the house, waiting for the next instruction. If he was told to attack he knew what to do.

"What on earth is this person doing there?" Constable Wood whispered to Mr Ted.

There was nothing in the briefing about people coming to the house or leaving it. There were no other police officers on duty around the house, just the two police dog teams. Constable Wood had been told at the briefing that the guests were all inside, and had been for hours. So who was this walking about outside the house? What were they doing there and what was their business? There was only one way to find out, and that was to challenge them. Before Constable Wood could utter a word they both noticed something else at the back of the house. In the dark, and with little light to see by, they could just make out the shape of a dog. A small dog, much smaller than Mr Ted, about ten times smaller in fact. It was very small with no tail and very short legs. They could also see now that the person was a woman, a small woman wearing a long coat and a headscarf. The little dog seemed to be with her because it was running around at her feet, not going very far and then going back to her.

"This is no burglar or thief," thought Constable Wood. "I'll have to handle this very carefully."

"Stand still! I am a police officer with a dog! Stay where you are or I will release the dog!"

The woman, looking startled, did as she was told and acknowledged Constable Wood by raising her right hand. Constable Wood walked up to her shining his torch as he approached. Mr Ted walked alongside him; he was off the lead and kept edging just one pace ahead of him and growling a deep growl as he went forward. One word from Constable Wood and Mr Ted was ready to charge forward. The little dog would not have been a distraction; he was focused only on the woman. She stepped backwards as she saw Mr Ted, and he took another step further forward.

"Heel Ted!" Constable Wood shouted.

"Stay absolutely still. Don't move!"

When they got to within three metres of her Constable Wood told Mr Ted to stay.

"What are you doing here, and what do you want?"

The woman spoke in a cultured and quiet voice, "One of the corgis wanted to go outside. He was getting quite restless I had to do something. I'm sorry if I have caused you any unnecessary alarm officer. That was not my intention."

"Okay so the corgi needed to go outside, but who are you?"

"I am........"

Just as she started speaking it suddenly dawned on Constable Wood who it was he was speaking to. He should have known as soon as he saw her. It was the Queen! Constable Wood offered his apologies at once.

"No need for an apology officer. I am very pleased to see that you and your companion are alert and doing your job. Well done and keep up the good work. We appreciate what you do here."

She called the corgi closer to her. As it ran back the little dog got close to Mr Ted. The two dogs hit it off straight away despite the huge difference in their sizes. Mr Ted stood high in the air above the corgi and was wagging his tail and it was clear too that the dogs liked each other. Constable Wood let Mr Ted off his lead and the two of them ran around on the lawn at the back of the big house until Her Majesty called her dog and went inside. They said goodnight to each other, and in she went.

A short while later Constable Wood went to the front of the house and met up with Constable Markham.

"You'll never guess who we've just met."

"Who?"

"It was the Queen and one of her corgis. They were just out getting some air, and the corgi needed to go outside. She was lovely, and the dogs got on very well together."

"Yeah right." said Constable Markham in a disbelieving tone of voice. "You think I'm going to fall for that one?"

The rest of that night and the following night nothing out of the ordinary happened at all. It was quiet inside and outside the mansion whilst Mr Ted kept guard. Constables Wood and Markham were told that the Royal party would be leaving the estate early the next morning to go back to London. As before they would search the garage and the car there to make sure everything was all right before the driver collected the car for the Queen. Then they were told to stay on duty to escort the Royal party in their cars back to the main road where they would be met by police traffic patrol cars who would escort the Queen on her way back to London. By 6 o'clock the searches were complete and the Queen's chauffeur arrived to pick up the Rolls Royce and take it to the front door of the mansion.

Constable Wood, in his best police uniform was near to the front door, with Mr Ted smartly groomed and on his lead, just in time to see Her Majesty leave the house. In the few steps that it took her to get to her car she looked around her and saw Constable Wood and Mr Ted. She smiled at them both and raised her hand in a gentle wave. Constable Wood saluted. The corgi ran behind her. The two dogs recognised each other straight away. After passing a glance at each other the little corgi jumped into the back of the car with the Queen. The Rolls Royce drove off at a regal and dignified pace along the long drive towards the gates of the mansion. Constable Wood and Mr Ted drove in front until they reached the gate safely and the escort was taken up by the traffic officers in their Range Rover police cars and off they went to London. That would not be the last time that Mr Ted saw the Queen.

Chapter Eight

Mr Ted goes to Church

A year later Constable Wood was told by Sergeant Fleming that he and Mr Ted were being sent to Amcester Cathedral in College Green, Amcester where the Queen was attending an Easter service. They were going with other police officers from police forces all over England to join together to make sure that the cathedral was safe and secure for the Queen whilst she was there. The day before the Royal visit Constable Wood and Mr Ted went to the Amcester police headquarters and reported for duty. Both Mr Ted and Constable Wood were excited about this change from routine.

They were in a party of several police dogs and handlers whose job, they were told by the Inspector in charge, was to search the inside of the cathedral and its grounds. They worked in teams in the empty cathedral all day and other police teams worked on

105

the outside in the grounds of the huge church. At the end of it all they were able to report back that there was nothing, nothing at all, that would harm anyone in any way, and that the cathedral was secured until the next day.

The next morning soon after 9 o'clock a crowd began to gather outside the cathedral. They were in a jubilant mood and excitedly looking forward to the Queen arriving for the Easter service. Constable Wood and Mr Ted's duties had changed from the searching that they had done the day before, to patrolling the area where the crowd were, making sure that nothing out of the ordinary happened, or that no harm could come to The Queen when she walked out from the cathedral to meet the people.

The Queen arrived at the cathedral in her Rolls Royce limousine, the same car that Mr Ted had searched a year before, and was greeted with a loud and welcoming cheer and lots of flag waving. There were children from the local schools in their hundreds, who had been allowed out to see the Queen. There were people from all walks of life there too, and by the time the Queen entered the cathedral there were several thousand outside. They were all behind barriers that had been put in place by the council, and allowed a safe area for the Queen to walk in. It also allowed everyone in the crowd to get a good view of her when she arrived and when she walked about after the service.

Suddenly a huge cheer went up from the crowd. All the children were shouting and waving their flags as she came out from the cathedral and began to walk in the street outside and along the rows of people. She stopped occasionally to talk to some of the children, and some of them presented her with flowers. The Queen was smiling and talking to the children, it was a beautiful warm sunny day.

Constable Wood and Mr Ted were at the back of the crowd looking from behind everyone. Right at the back Constable Wood saw a scruffy man who was behaving a bit strangely. He was wearing an old and torn coat, blue jeans that were dirty and ripped at the knees, and a pair of dirty white trainer shoes. He was looking around him and checking his pockets all the time, and he looked alarmed when Constable Wood and Mr Ted started to walk towards him. Constable Wood knew that there was something not quite right about this man, but he didn't know what it was. He had nothing to go on just a gut feeling that something wasn't quite right.

The crowd were enjoying the Royal visit, and anything that Constable Wood did next, if he wasn't very careful, could spoil everything. On the other hand if he didn't act quickly it might be too late. Now the man was staring at Mr Ted. He was getting even more agitated at the sight of a trained police dog and his handler approaching him. When they got to within five metres of him he broke away from the crowd and ran off as fast as he could away from Constable Wood and Mr Ted up a grass bank and down the other side, out of the view of the crowd and the Queen. Mr Ted was on his lead as they ran after him.

"Stand still or I will release the dog!"

The man looked over his shoulder back towards Mr Ted but kept on running. He heard the call to stop, but ignored it and ran even faster towards a nearby railway bridge. Mr Ted was straining on his lead, running ahead of Constable Wood barking as he ran. He told Ted to be quiet and shouted at the man again telling him to stop or he would release Mr Ted.

The man ran onto the railway bridge just as a fast train was passing underneath. He stopped in the middle and faced Constable Wood and Mr Ted who were a few metres behind him. He pulled a large knife from his pocket.

"Stay back copper or you'll get this."

He waved the knife menacingly towards Constable Wood, and just as he said that Constable Wood could see a group of children behind the man walking towards the bridge. The man hadn't seen them yet. He was only interested in watching the policeman and his dog. The knife was big, very big and Constable Wood thought he would use it in order to escape. Mr Ted could see the knife too, and was looking for a way to attack the man and get it from him. The children were getting closer, not realising what was going on. Constable Wood had to act quickly.

"Put that knife down now!"

"Leave me alone. I mean it, I'll stab you if you come near me."

"What are you doing here anyway? Why have you got that knife?"

"I'm going to get the Queen, and you won't stop me!"

109

The man turned around and saw the children, and started to walk towards them.

"I'll take one of those," he said as a made towards them. The children started screaming and ran away in all directions.

Constable Wood knew that he had no more time to waste talking. Mr Ted was straining on the lead, leaping forward as far as the lead would allow him and barking wildly. He knew what was coming next. He knew that at any moment he would be released by Constable Wood and his job would be to attack the man with the knife and get it from him.

"Attack Ted! Attack!"

Constable Wood released Ted from his lead and sent him on his way. Mr Ted was running at full speed. The scruffy man, despite his threats, turned to run away from Mr Ted, and just as he got close to the children, with his knife still in his hand, Mr Ted came up behind him and leapt into the air with his mouth open wide and teeth showing. He grabbed the arm with the knife in it with his teeth, shaking the knife from the man's grip. The force of Mr Ted hitting him made the man fall onto his face with Mr Ted holding onto his arm all the time. Constable Wood was right

110

behind Mr Ted. When he got up close he picked up the knife and called Mr Ted to heel. Mr Ted let go of the man and stood beside Constable Wood barking at the man. Constable Wood handcuffed him with his hands behind his back.

"You're under arrest!"

He marched him back to his police patrol van with Mr Ted keeping a close watch. The children on the other side of the bridge looked on in amazement when they saw Mr Ted go into action, and cheered when the man was made to drop his knife by Mr Ted.

The Queen and most of the crowd watching her knew nothing about Mr Ted's spectacular arrest. They took the man quietly away to the police station.

Constable Wood knelt down and put his arm around Mr Ted. "That could have been nasty Mr Ted. You did well again, good boy."

Chapter Nine

More Burglars are rounded up by Mr Ted at the Rugby Club

Constable Wood and Mr Ted were patrolling as usual in their white police patrol van, it was like Mr Ted's home for at least eight hours on most days, whether it was summer or winter, it provided comfort and security for Mr Ted and he became very fond of it, and his space in the back right behind Constable Wood. From there he had a view out through the caged interior, which was especially made for him. He could also turn around and see out of the back window and watch what was going on behind. If, as quite often happened, the police headquarters called them up on the radio to attend an incident; Constable Wood always put on the blue flashing police light and turned on the siren, which was always a signal to Mr Ted that they were on their way to more adventure. He didn't know which way to look to get the best view. He turned around and around in the back of the van looking forwards and backwards as many times as he could on the journey, at the same time barking very loudly. Mr Ted spinning around like that always resulted in a whipped up storm of loose dog hair being sent around the van as it sped along and most of it, or so it seemed to Eddie Wood, always landed on his clean police uniform. He often thought that after one of these high speed jaunts he looked more like a German Shepherd than Mr Ted did!

Constable Wood and Mr Ted had just started another night shift in the middle of a week of night work, when a call came over the radio. Mr Ted's ears pricked up as he listened to the call.

"Please go silently to Stockwood Rugby Club, the burglar alarm has activated."

Constable Wood knew that he had just ten minutes to get to the club before the alarm bells on the outside started to ring and alert the burglars. Sometimes there were no burglars. Burglar alarms could be set off by the wind blowing a door open, or a power cut or even a mistake by the manager not setting the alarm properly when he locked up, and this used to happen quite a lot.

Anyway, if Constable Wood was to give himself and Mr Ted any chance of catching them, he thought he had better get there pretty quickly. He put on the blue flashing light and started to speed as fast and as safely as he could on his way to the rugby club. Mr Ted sensed what was going on and set about doing his routine in the back of the van by turning around and around as if he was in a tumble dryer or washing machine on top speed setting, spreading his loose hair all over Constable Wood.

They got to the club within five minutes; luckily they were not that far away when the call came. On the way down the oak tree lined driveway to the clubhouse Constable Wood switched off all his lights, blue light and driving lights, and glided as quietly as he could drive to as close as he dare to the club house. He switched off the engine and got out of the van closing the door quietly behind him. As he got Mr Ted out of the back of the van and put him onto his lead he could hear the wind blowing in the trees that surrounded the club house, and could see leaves and small twigs being blown off the trees above them in the wind. As they walked the last few metres towards the club house he could see that a fire escape door on the side of the building was banging open and closed in the strong wind. The building was in total darkness and there were no lights on the outside either.

Constable Wood had almost made his mind up that this was going to be a false alarm. He thought that the door had probably not been closed properly, and that the strong winds had blown the door open causing the burglar alarm to go off. With that thought in his mind he approached the swinging door with Mr Ted.

"Well we're here now; we might as well do the job properly."

He sat Mr Ted just inside the door, took his lead off and whispered to him to stay by his side.

"This is the police! Show yourself now or I will release my police dog!"

What happened next startled both Constable Wood and Mr Ted. From inside the club house and off to their left came the unmistakable sound of running feet, breaking glasses and someone crashing into tables and chairs in the dark.

"Stand still or I *will* release my dog!"

They heard more crashing about in the dark.

"Find them Ted."

Mr Ted took off into the darkness inside the club bar room; Constable Wood couldn't see what was happening but could hear two different voices shouting, Mr Ted barking and then a very loud crash of breaking glass coming from his left. Constable Wood looked in the direction of the sound and saw pieces of broken glass and a chair flying outwards from a window at the side of the building closely followed by a man who was flying head first through the broken window. He was followed closely by a second man who was holding a heavy bag of things he had stolen from the club. Both men ran one after the other towards the rugby field. They ran between the rugby posts nearest the club house and out across the playing field towards the other goal posts. Mr Ted flew out through the same window chasing after them. He looked mean and angry and was barking after them. One of them looked over his shoulder at the pursuing police dog.

Constable Wood shouted "Stand still!"

The man with the bag did just that. Constable Wood ran after Mr Ted who was circling the man barking at him, holding him there until Constable Wood got to him seconds later.

"Well done Ted, now stop him." pointing to the second man.

Constable Wood took the bag from the burglar and handcuffed him whilst Mr Ted set off after the other one who by now had got to within a few metres of the other goal posts. It was no challenge for Mr Ted. He had trained on the sports ground at the dog training school. To see a man running away from him onto a rugby field and being told to stop him reminded him of his training field. The burglar stood no chance as long as Mr Ted could see him, and as long as he stayed on the field he was going to be caught, but still he kept on running. Mr Ted got right up behind him and launched himself at the running burglar and landed on his back with his front paws. The weight and speed of the police dog knocked him off his feet. He fell to the ground with a thud face down in the wet grass and mud, knocking the breath out of him, with Mr Ted standing on his back barking in his ear. He didn't dare move or say a word. Mr Ted held him there in that position until Constable Wood got to him and handcuffed the two burglars together.

"Well done again Ted. I don't remember us being trained to jump on people's backs, but it works."

Chapter Ten

Mr Ted Goes for a Midnight Dip

That same windy night turned out to be a busy night for Constable Wood and Mr Ted. It was a busy night for the burglars too! They had not been on patrol for very much longer when they were called to a burglary at a house in Oakley Road, Hawkridge. The owner had made an emergency call to the police.

"There's someone downstairs! I heard a window being broken. Come quick. Help me."

"Control to Constable Wood. Go to 29 Oakley Road Hawkridge. The occupiers report a burglary in progress at their home. We are sending other patrols too."

"We're on the way. We should be no more than five minutes."

Constable Wood pressed the accelerator and off they sped in the direction of Oakley Road, racing around the streets of north

Hawkridge one after the other until they came into Oakley Road. As Constable Wood drove along the tree lined avenue, with its detached and semi detached houses facing each other in a neat row on either side, he could see the blue flashing lights of the police cars that had got there before him. When he pulled up and got Mr Ted out of the back of the van, there were already two or three policemen and women walking up to the front door. As Mr Ted and Constable Wood walked onto the drive the front bedroom window flew open and the house owner leaned out of the window.

"He's in the back garden! He's just got out of the back window and is in the garden!"

Constable Wood told the other police officers to stand still and released Mr Ted from his lead and sent him around the side of the house to the back garden.

"Find him Ted."

Mr Ted raced forward with Constable Wood running behind him, as the man in the upstairs window shouted "Mind the swi…." just as Mr Ted ran onto the lawn at the back of the house. At least it looked like a lawn. In fact, it was the green net cover of the outdoor swimming pool and the way it was stretched out over the pool it looked to Mr Ted just like a grass lawn in the darkness. Constable Wood got there a few paces behind Mr Ted to see him floundering about on the green cover. He couldn't walk or run on it because it was sinking. He couldn't swim either because the water wasn't deep enough in the net. As he struggled to get out or swim, his legs were getting tangled in it. He could see the dark figure of the burglar climbing over the fence at the bottom of the fifty metre garden and he wanted to get after him. The net was pulling him down. What a tangled mess!

Neither Constable Wood nor Mr Ted had been in a situation like this before. What a mess, Ted was stuck in the pool and the burglar was getting away.

"So that's what the man was shouting from the window, he did try to warn us about the pool. But the warning was a bit too late, wasn't it Ted?"

What was even more annoying to Constable Wood was that somehow the burglar had managed to run around the side of the pool and miss it all together. Constable Wood had to think quickly if he was to save Mr Ted, the more he struggled, the more he got tangled up, and the more he sank into the water. He got alongside the pool and stretched out his right arm and grabbed Mr Ted by the loose skin on the back of his neck. With a firm grip, he managed to pull Mr Ted to the side and helped him get himself out of the pool. A soaking wet German Shepherd is very heavy, but the combined strength of the two of them got him safely to the side. Mr Ted was pleased to be out of there and did what all wet dogs do, shook himself dry! Constable Wood, was still kneeling beside Ted and didn't get out of the way of Ted's doggy shake in time, and got soaking wet too.

"Thanks Ted. I needed that!"

Very quickly they both turned their attention back to the fleeing burglar who by now had got over the fence at the bottom of the garden and two more garden fences besides and had disappeared from view.

Constable Wood pointed towards the bottom of the garden, as if Mr Ted needed telling, he was on his way.

"Find him Ted!"

Mr Ted raced off and leapt the two metre fence like a thoroughbred race horse running in the Grand National. He quickly searched the garden next door using his super sensitive police dog nose and picked up the trail. It led to the next garden and then the next. Mr Ted leapt over each of the fences until he landed on the lawn in the house three houses away from where they had started the chase. Constable Eddie Wood could hear him rushing around the bushes in the garden, and he could hear him breathing as he clambered over the last fence to join him in the search.

It was clear to Constable Wood that the man they had been chasing was nearby because Mr Ted kept checking the fences, and he was showing no interest in them. That could only mean one thing, he must still be in the garden somewhere, but where? Mr Ted put his nose close to the ground, he needed no instruction from Constable Wood, he knew what he was looking for and he was using all his natural ability and his police search training to find him and he was getting close. The scent going into his nose was as fresh and strong as the smell of freshly cut grass in the summer; only in this case it was the fresh scent of a man on the grass lawn at the back of a house, and that man was a stranger and didn't belong there. Worse than that, he was a burglar and on the run from the police. Mr Ted, working hard, moving very fast, with his nose to the ground, did a full circuit of the garden and lifted his head as he went past the wooden garden shed. He sniffed at the door and ran all around the shed and back to the door. He stood still and barked at it, telling Constable Wood that he had found the burglar. Constable Wood told Mr Ted to be quiet, and opened the shed door and lying crouched in the corner at the far end they both saw the burglar. Mr Ted wanted to go in after him, but Constable Wood held him back.

"Are you going to come quietly?"

"Yes I will. Please keep that dog away from me, please."

"Come out of there then. The dog won't come near you if you behave."

Nervously and slowly he came out. Mr Ted watched him very closely as they both took him back into the street. The other officers were waiting to take him to the police station.

"Well done Mr Ted. What a night. Let's go back to Wavehill and get some food and rest for you."

Chapter Eleven

Mr Ted to the Rescue

Mr Ted and Constable Eddie Wood were on patrol as usual one sunny morning in Tennyson Road in Hawkridge. They were walking side by side enjoying the walk and the quiet of the streets in the early morning when Constable Wood noticed smoke coming from the bedroom window of one of the long row of terraced house that spread out along the pavement in front of them. Constable Wood ran up to the house. He banged loudly on the front door, which was right on the pavement. At the same time he called the fire brigade using his police radio. It was obvious to him from the black billowing smoke pouring out of the bedroom window that the house was on fire! He couldn't waste any time if he was going to be able to help anyone trapped inside.

Even though he knew that the fire brigade were on the way Constable Wood kept banging on the door. Eventually, a man and woman with two young children came running out of the front door on to the street.

"Is that all of you out? Is anyone left inside?"

"This is all of us, there is no one else." the man said, rubbing his eyes and picking up one of the small children, his daughter Emma.

"Where's Baker? He's still inside!" she shrieked.

"Who's Baker?"

"He's our dog." said the dad, "and she's right. He must be still inside."

Both the children were crying and shouting for Baker. Smoke was starting to come out through the open front door as well as the upstairs windows. Constable Wood could hear the sirens of the approaching fire engines. His first thoughts were that he could go into the house and find the dog, and then as quickly as he thought that he dismissed it from his mind, thinking instead that the fire brigade would soon be there and they could get him. They were trained and equipped to do rescues. He looked into the house through the open door again. He thought he could hear the sound of Baker barking from inside. Mr Ted pricked his ears up too, there was no mistake he could hear Baker's urgent call for help. As each second ticked by the chances of Baker getting out safe before the smoke or fire got him were getting less and less. He had to be got out and into the fresh air or he might die in the house.

Constable Wood took another look inside. He looked up and down the street again for the fire brigade. He made up his mind to go in and try to find Baker.

"Wait here Mr Ted." He said as he dropped his lead next to him. Mr Ted looked up at him wondering what was going to happen next.

Just as he took a deep breath stepped across the threshold, Mr Ted rushed passed him and headed straight along the narrow hallway to the back of the house, passing a door to the front room on his left and pushing open the door to the kitchen where he could hear Baker. He'd been pushing at the door, but all he was doing was pushing it closed all the time. As the door flew open Mr Ted stepped inside and saw Baker straightaway. He was shaking, barking and very frightened. Mr Ted used his mouth to take hold of Baker by the scruff of his neck and quickly carried him out into the hallway where he met Constable Wood who took Baker from him. They all quickly ran out onto the street. The whole rescue was over in seconds, Baker was fine and his family were delighted to see that he was safe.

The fire brigade arrived at the same time and quickly put the fire out. It was an electrical fault in the airing cupboard that started the fire. They soon had that under control, and once they had done that, apart from a lot of smoke damage and smell, the rest of the house was saved.

After the family had made a great fuss of Baker they put him on the pavement and he and Mr Ted spent some time together wagging their tails. They looked like they were talking to each other. Mr Ted looked pleased with himself. When the fire brigade left they all went back into the house and thanked Constable Wood and Mr Ted for getting them up and out. They all said a special thank you to Mr Ted for rescuing Baker. Constable Wood and Mr Ted said goodbye promising to see them all again. They set off walking along the road towards the police station, the pair of them smelling of smoke and thinking that's enough excitement and adventure for one day.

Once the pair got back to their police van, Constable Wood drove them off to the mansion at Broughton House and the lake there. He parked the van beside the lake, and let Mr Ted out. As soon as Mr Ted saw the water he jumped in and swam around. He liked swimming, and this time he was getting the smoke out of his coat too. He got out of the water and searched around on the bank for a while until he found a stick. He picked it up and ran up to Constable Wood and sat in front of him with the stick in his mouth wagging his tail. He wanted to play.

"I know what you want."

Constable Wood threw the stick into the lake, Mr Ted chased after it. Picking it up in his mouth he swam back to the bank and sat in front of Constable Wood again. Once more he threw the stick for him and Mr Ted chased it again, and again, and again.

After they had played this game of fetch for a while Constable Wood rubbed him down with a towel that he carried in the van and gave his coat a brushing then and there by the side of the lake. Mr Ted felt and looked much cleaner for it. Constable Wood got changed when they got back to the police station, and they were fit for duty again and off they went once again on their patrol.

They saw lots of Baker and his family after that day, often meeting him in the road when he was out for a walk, and the two dogs always knew each other whenever they met

Chapter Twelve

Mr Ted makes friends with Churchill the Police Horse

Patrol work was routine for Constable Wood and Mr Ted. They spent a great deal of time just patrolling the streets and roads, in the van or on foot, waiting for a call over the radio. They always had two days off every week, and at least once a month they got together with the other police dogs and their handlers to practise the skills that they had all learnt at training school. Sometimes on these monthly training days they met up with the police horses and their riders for joint training days. It was on these training days that Mr Ted and Police Horse Churchill first got to know each other. It was whilst working with Churchill that Mr Ted remembered his early days on Mr and Mrs Wilson's farm, and when he lived with John Edwards the milkman, and Churchill reminded him of the good times he had had with other animals there before he became a police dog.

Most police horses are huge animals, and so was Churchill, A big grey horse whose rider was Constable Georgina Kennedy. Georgina and Churchill had been together for over five years working in Walthamshire. In the saddle, high up on Churchill's back Constable Kennedy could see a lot more than the other police patrols. Not only that, she could be seen too.

A few weeks after the fire at Baker's house, Mr Ted and Constable Wood were called to fields on farm land at Wisburn on the Duke of Waltham's estate. There they met up with four police horses and their riders, and three more police dogs and handlers. The horses and their riders had all arrived there in a big police horse lorry, driven on most days by Constable Kennedy. It was lunchtime by the time they all got together. They were met by Sergeant Fleming. He gathered the men and women together to tell them that he wanted them to look for an elderly man who was missing from his home in the nearby village of Milton Queens. He had left his house at breakfast time to go to the shop for a newspaper, but he did not return home and after an hour his wife had called her neighbour to help her look for him. She was worried because he was a bit confused and she thought he might have got lost. Sergeant Fleming also said that the neighbours had been looking for him all morning and found out that he had never got to the shop and no one had seen him since he left his house earlier in the day. He had never done anything like this before; his family were worried and called the police for help. It had been raining hard all day and was still raining. It was cold in the biting wind too, and there was real concern for the man who had been missing for half a day without any explanation. No one had seen him, and it seemed as though he had just disappeared.

Sergeant Fleming asked the constables to get their dogs and horses and search the surrounding farmland. He told them to do the searching as quickly and thoroughly as possible. He had split the area up into four equal size sections, and split the horse and dog teams equally so that each horse and rider worked with a police dog and handler. Constable Wood was allocated to work with Constable Georgina Kennedy. They both knew that when Churchill and Mr Ted saw each other they would be pleased to be working together on this important work.

Constable Wood got Mr Ted from the van, he put him on his lead, took his tracking harness and an extra long tracking rope lead with them and together they walked over to the lorry just in time to see Georgina leading Churchill down the ramp and watched as he was saddled up. Mr Ted kept pulling on his lead, wagging his tail and yelping at the sight of Churchill. The big horse stood still while he was having his saddle put on, but constantly looked in Mr Ted's direction with a sparkle in his eye. Constable Kennedy got up onto Churchill and once she was ready she asked Churchill to head in the direction of the fields that they had to search. The other teams had also gone off to the areas they had been given and began the search. If the missing man was in these fields then these combined police horse and dog teams, which were trained in searches like this, would surely find him. The question was, would they find him fit and well and return him safely to his family?

Earlier Sergeant Fleming in his briefing had told them that he wanted them to search any open ground such as fields and woods around the man's house and then report back to him if they found him or not. They were told that they were looking for a man in his seventies who had grey hair, walked with a walking stick, and, despite the fact that it was raining hard, when he left his house his coat was still in the house hanging up in the hall. He was dressed only in a shirt and woollen jumper which was green, a pair of grey trousers and black shoes. They were also told to waste no time in getting started if they were to find the man quickly.

Churchill, with Constable Kennedy on his back, Mr Ted and Constable Wood set off for the fields that they had been told to search. They soon arrived at the field gate just outside the village and Constable Wood opened it to let Churchill through and once they were all inside he closed the gate behind them.

"I tell you what Georgina, you ride over the open fields and I'll go with Mr Ted into that wooded area over there. I'll get Mr Ted to search on his own in the woods, and we'll meet up here again in an hour."

"All right, let's get on with it. The quicker we get started the quicker we might find the poor man." Constable Kennedy said thoughtfully.

She gave the big grey horse a gentle nudge and he trotted off over the fields at a steady pace with the wind and rain driving into his face. Constable Kennedy could see a long way from the top of Churchill, but so far there was no sign of the missing man.

Constable Wood and Mr Ted got to the woods which ran along the roadside and he released Mr Ted from his lead.

"Seek."

Mr Ted, as usual, didn't need telling twice; off he went with his nose to the ground searching for any human scent as he went. Constable Wood followed him through the trees and encouraged him to work as they went along, keeping his eyes open for any sign of the man himself too.

"Come on Ted. If anyone can find this man you should be able to."

From time to time he could see Churchill and Georgina working in the fields. They both had their heads down against the driving rain. It was wet too in the trees, but the wind was nowhere near as bad as outside in the fields. They had been searching for about half an hour when Constable Kennedy came galloping over to the woods on Churchill shouting for Eddie Wood as she got closer. Mr Ted and Constable Wood could hear the thunder of

Churchill's hooves on the ground, and they could hear Constable Kennedy shouting at them.

"I've been calling you on the radio, why didn't you answer me? I've found him, but he's stuck and I can't get him out on my own. Come quickly!"

"I don't think these radios are working in amongst these trees. Sorry about that Georgina. Where is he? Let's go."

Churchill led the way across the fields followed by Mr Ted who was running free alongside him. Constable Wood was running behind across three large fields of short grass land until they came to a brook that blocked their path. Constable Kennedy and Churchill turned left and followed the brook for a hundred metres or so with Mr Ted and Eddie Wood right behind them, until they came to a small wooden bridge that ran over the brook between two fields.

"He was here in the water. I'm sure he was here, but he's gone!"

The water was rushing through the ditch. There was no sign of the man now. Even from on top of Churchill Constable Kennedy couldn't see him.

"All right Georgina. I know what to do." He called Mr Ted to his side.

"Ted, seek!"

Mr Ted put his nose to the ground at first searching for scent. Then he lifted his head and ran off along the bank. He ran faster as the scent in his nose grew stronger. Constable Wood could tell that Mr Ted was on to something and ran after him.

"Come on Georgina. He must be along here somewhere."

Mr Ted stopped and started barking at something in the water. There, below him in the water, hanging on to a branch on the side, was the missing man. He was almost totally covered by fast flowing water; just his head and arms were visible above it. The water looked very dangerous indeed and it was nearly over the top of the slippery bank, and very nearly over the top of the man! He was in great danger, one slip and he would surely go under. Constables Wood and Kennedy had to think and act fast if they stood any chance at all of saving him. He looked tired and weak; the water was pulling at him. He was pleading with the officers to help him.

"Help me please. I can't hold on much longer!"

To get into the water looked very dangerous it was flowing so fast. But what else could they do? Thinking quickly what to do next Constable Wood told Mr Ted to stay on the bank as he took the dog's tracking harness and long rope lead from his shoulder and unravelled it.

"Tie this end around Churchill's saddle. When I give you the signal will you and Churchill pull us out please?"

Constable Kennedy quickly tied the rope around the saddle and watched as Eddie Wood tied the other end around his own waist. He dropped and slipped down the bank into the water alongside the man.

"Keep hold of that branch until I tell you to let go." he said to the man as he felt the strength of the water trying to pull him under.

The rope between him and Churchill became tight as the big horse took the strain. He put his arms around the man's waist and told him to let go of the branch. At first he couldn't do it. He felt that if he let go that he would be sucked away by the water, even though Constable Wood was holding on tightly to his waist.

"Let go! We've got to get out of this water before it's too late. Let go now!"

The man relaxed his grip on the branch and Constable Wood shouted above the noise of the water to Georgina and Churchill to pull them out. The great horse pulled backwards, as Georgina encouraged him. He took the weight of the two soaking wet men. Slowly but surely, with great strength and determination he pulled the two of them out of the grip of the water, up the slippery bank and onto the muddy field and to safety.

Georgina Kennedy radioed to Sergeant Fleming to say that they had found the man and that he was cold and wet and needed urgent medical assistance. She also told the sergeant where they were and that they would get the man to the road and asked for an ambulance to be there. They were a long way from the road and too far away for the man to walk. He was weak and tired from his ordeal in the water, and getting weaker by the minute. Having got him this far, and saved him from drowning in the brook, the two Constables were determined not to let his condition get any worse. He was already soaking wet. The cold rain was still falling as they tried to work out how they would get him to the road and the safety and warmth of an ambulance. Constable Kennedy had an idea.

"If you can help me get him up onto Churchill," she said to Eddie Wood, "we can get him across these fields and to the road."

She encouraged Churchill to get down low onto his knees; he seemed to sense what was going on and lowered his huge body nearer to the ground. The two constables lifted him onto Churchill's back. Then Constable Kennedy got onto Churchill's back behind the man, took hold of the horse's reins and told him to stand up again. Churchill raised himself to his full height, shook himself gently, and moved slowly forward when told to by Constable Kennedy. Then he broke into a trot towards the road, with Mr Ted and Constable Wood running alongside them. On the way they could hear the sirens of the ambulance getting louder as it got nearer to the field gate.

"Is he all right Georgina? It's freezing."

"He's shivering, but the ambulance is getting close. He'll be all right in there."

The ambulance and Churchill got to the gate at the same time as the man's wife. She was crying with relief, but at the same time worried about his condition. She watched as the man was taken from Churchill's back by the ambulance crew, put onto a stretcher and lifted into the dry and warm inside of the ambulance. She got in too as he was quickly taken off to hospital with the sirens and blue lights on.

"You should have gone with them Eddie. You're soaking wet."

"I'll be all right. Let's get back to headquarters as quick as we can."

They made their way back to the horse lorry and dog van, dried off as best they could there, and straightaway drove to the police headquarters where Churchill and Mr Ted went to the stable block and in the dry and warm of the building, they were both quickly dried off by Constables Kennedy and Wood. Churchill was led into his stable and before Constable Kennedy could close the door Mr Ted pushed past her and stood next to Churchill who dropped his head to Mr Ted's level and the two of them touched noses.

"Those two look all right together. Let's leave them there for a while and go and get ourselves cleaned up and have some tea shall we?"

Once he got to the hospital the man was seen straight away by the doctors in Accident and Emergency. He was kept in overnight for observations, but allowed home the next day. He won't do that again. Hopefully!

Chapter Thirteen

Snakes Alive Mr Ted. What was That?

Dogs and horses, and some farm animals were all familiar fellow creatures to Mr Ted. When he was very young he was used to farm animals and enjoyed their company. Later, when he became a police dog he trained with other dogs, then police horses, and during the course of his work he met other animals too, like the squirrels and rabbits that were always in the fields and woods where they trained and worked. But nothing had prepared him for an encounter he had with a most unusual animal when he and Constable Wood were called late one night to the house next door to the Labrador Baker, whose house had caught on fire a few months before, when Mr Ted and he had met for the first time.

They were there because the family in the house had been woken up by some loud banging noises. It sounded to them as if someone was in their loft and they called the police. Constable Wood and Mr Ted pulled up quietly outside the house in their police patrol van and he ware met at the door by an anxious Gary Williams and his wife.

"We can hear someone in the loft. We've only been home about an hour and had just got off to sleep when this banging from the loft woke us up."

"Is there any sign of a break in?"

"No. Nothing that we've seen." said Gary. "We can't work out how they've got in there, but there's definitely someone up there. We can hear them walking about. I daren't go up there."

"All right Gary, I'll have a look. Where's the hatch?"

They went upstairs leaving Mr Ted in the back of the van outside on the road. He looked out of the back window of the van and could see Baker's face looking at him from under the curtains in the front window of his house. Mr Ted wanted to get out of the van and join Constable Wood, and he would soon get his wish.

Constable Wood listened for a while at the top of the stairs, right under the loft hatch. He heard nothing at first, and then there it was, a loud bang, just as if someone had knocked something over in the loft.

"Out you come, it's the police. Come down now!"

It went very quiet, but no one appeared at the hatch. Then the silence was broken by another bang. Constable Wood, thinking that there must be someone or something in the loft, got a chair from the bedroom and stood on it whilst he lifted the loft hatch out of the way leaving an opening in the ceiling big enough for him to look into. He took his torch and shone it into the darkness of the loft.

"I know you are here. Come out now or I'll come and get you. I have a police dog with me and I'll put him in here."

It was quiet and there was no more movement, nor could he see anyone. What he could see was some boxes, piles of books, some pieces of furniture, a pram and an old television set. He got down off the chair and told Gary that he was going to get Mr Ted to have a look in there. He soon got back to the landing with Mr Ted on his lead. Mr Ted sensed that he was getting involved in something, but didn't know what; he looked interested, but puzzled. He soon worked out that Constable Wood was worried about the dark space at the top of a ladder that led up to the ceiling.

Constable Wood shouted one more warning into the loft and when he got no answer he encouraged Mr Ted to climb the ladder. Mr Ted got up the ladder and pulled himself into the opening of the loft and took in the scents and smells around him. Constable Wood climbed up behind him and shone his torch into the darkness.

"Seek Ted."

Ted began searching as Constable Wood encouraged him and watched him working. It wasn't long before Mr Ted's hair stood up on his back, a sure sign that he had seen something. He stood there staring into the darkness behind some boxes. He looked at Constable Wood, then looked back and started barking to let Constable Wood know that he had found someone, or something.

"Come out now! Show yourself and I'll call the dog off!"

Nothing, just silence and no movement, except the noise of Mr Ted barking.

"Quiet Ted! Come out I said. Let me see you!"

Still there was no movement. Ted started barking once more and left what he was looking at to come closer to Constable Wood. He sent him back and as he was getting closer to the spot in the loft where he had been barking both Mr Ted and Constable Wood heard a loud hissing sound, just like the hissing sound of steam coming out of a steam iron. Ted barked even louder.

"What on earth was that Ted"

Mr Ted could see it. It was staring straight at him. To Ted it looked threatening and he had no idea what it was.

He shouted once or twice more for the stranger to show himself as he got closer to Ted. He shone his torch behind the boxes, and there in the beam he saw it. A huge three metre long snake! It was a giant South American Anaconda hissing loudly with its mouth open wide enough to show his sharp fangs. Constable Wood had only ever seen one in the zoo, or on television. He had never been this close to one before, and he didn't like it. It looked terrifying with its head held high, and mouth wide open, tongue moving in and out, and hissing loudly. He looked like he could strike out any second and bite him or Mr Ted. It was like being in a bad dream with a fierce monster in it from which there was no escape, feeling as if he was frozen to the spot not being able to get out of the way.

The police dog handler decided that it was best to get out of the way of this huge beast; Mr Ted looked like he would stand his ground, and fight it. Constable Wood started to walk backwards very slowly, trying not to make any sudden movements in case the snake attacked. He knew Mr Ted was in danger too. Mr Ted was very brave to stand there facing the snake and barking at it, but Constable Wood sensed that the snake might be too quick, even for Mr Ted. He called him away, and together they backed off, as they did, much to his relief, they saw the snake turn and slide into the darkness in the opposite direction.

"That was a close thing Mr Ted. You wouldn't want to get tangled up in a fight with that."

Constable Wood got down out of the loft helping Mr Ted on the ladder as he went. He closed the loft hatch door behind them and was met by Gary on the landing.

"I think we have found out what's making the noise up there. It's a giant snake. How did it get in there?"

"I've no idea said Gary," as his wife screamed and ran down the stairs to get as far away as possible from the loft and the snake that was on the loose in there.

"I don't know," said Gary. "It's not ours. I've no idea how it got there."

Constable Wood went outside to the street to get to the police van to put Mr Ted safely inside. They were met by Baker the Labrador and his family from next door.

"You don't own a snake do you?" said Constable Wood to the man, "only there's one in the loft in there, and we don't know whose it is and how it got there."

"No, not me," he said with surprise in his voice, "but hang on a minute. I saw a van go to number twenty six a couple of days ago and the men in it got a big box out of it and delivered it to the house. On the box it had the words *Reptiles – Handle with care.* That might be something to do with it."

Constable Wood put Mr Ted into the van and went to number twenty six where he knocked loudly on the door. He had to knock again before anyone answered, and when they did it was a man who looked surprised to see a policeman standing there at his front door.

"I'm sorry to disturb you, but I have reason to believe that you might have a snake here in the house and I wondered if I could see it please."

"Of course officer," said the man, "but why do you need to see my snake?"

"I'll tell you when I see it. Where is it?"

"Come inside. It's in its tank in the back room."

The two men walked through the house into the back room where the man switched on the light and there on the floor in the middle of the room was a large glass sided tank, about the size of a bath, with a lid on it, the lid was only half covering the tank and there was no sign of the snake, it was empty.

"Oh my goodness! Where's he gone? He was here this afternoon; I'm only looking after him for my brother for a few days while he's away on business. He told me he would be no trouble and would stay quietly in the tank until he came to get him. Where is he?"

"I think it's him in the loft of a house down the road. There's a three metre snake there and it's not theirs."

"That'll be him. He won't hurt anyone, but I can't handle him, and my brother is in France and won't be back for another couple of days."

Constable Wood called the police control room on his radio and told the operator what was going on and said that he needed help to get the snake back safely into its tank. The police control room contacted the reptile house at nearby Chiltern Zoo, and the night duty reptile keeper agreed to come to Tennyson Road to help catch the snake.

An hour later he was there with two of his assistants. They went into Gary's house after they got a full description of the snake from Constable Wood and the man at number twenty six. They went into the loft and quickly found it. The reptile keeper, who was very experienced in snake handling, and a good job that he was, picked it up and put it over his shoulders.

"Come on my beauty. Where were you going then? We'll look after you now."

He carried it out of the loft, down the stairs and out into their waiting zoo van, where they put it safely into a tank. As the keeper went past Mr Ted's van the snake hissed at him and he barked at the snake as he was carried by. There didn't seem much hope that Mr Ted and the hissing snake would ever become friends, and that suited Mr Ted just fine.

Constable Wood explained to Gary and his wife that the noises the heard were definitely the snake and nothing else, there were no burglars. Somehow it had got into the loft of number twenty six and made his way through the lofts of the terraced houses until it got to Gary's house where it tried to settle down for the night. Constable Wood reassured them that there were no more snakes, there was only ever one of them, and he was in the van on the way to the zoo for safe keeping until his owner came home from France. The snake would never be coming to visit Tennyson Road again.

After that snake adventure Constable Wood and Mr Ted carried on their patrol, but not before saying hello again to Baker. Constable Wood got Mr Ted out of the van and the two dogs spent a few minutes on the pavement together wagging their tails, looking at each other and speaking to each other with excited low barking. Although we'll never know, Constable Wood was pretty sure that Mr Ted was telling Baker all about finding the monster snake in the dark loft, and coming face to face with a wide open hissing mouth. Constable Wood called Mr Ted to him; said goodbye to those in the street, including Baker and off they went in the van together.

"Well done Mr Ted, what would we have done without you?"

Chapter Fourteen

Mr Ted Investigates Some Strange Country Noises

Constable Wood and Mr Ted had been called upon to do some pretty unusual things when they were on patrol. There was no doubt too that they would face other unknown adventures during their patrols which would be different to anything they had ever done before. The training that they had been given had always helped them in the past, and there was no reason to suppose that it wouldn't in the future. When they were called to the country to investigate some strange and unexplained screaming noises they embarked on yet another of their police dog adventures.

It was about one o'clock one warm night when the police headquarters started to get a number of telephone calls from the residents of Standon village just outside Hawkridge, where a few hundred people live in their houses, or on the few farms that are scattered along the long and winding road that runs through it.

People were calling the police to say that they had been woken up by the sound of screaming. It was loud screaming, just as if someone was hurt and in pain. The calls were coming in from all over the village, and every one of the callers were asked if they could tell where the screams were coming from, and they all seemed to agree that it was from the general direction of All Saints Church, the main gate of which was on a sharp bend in the road and right next to Swallow Farm.

Constable Wood and Mr Ted were sent to investigate and to report back to headquarters with what they find. They were already in Marsh Road in Hawkridge, and at that time of night there was very little traffic on the road and they were able to get to All Saints Church in about five minutes from when they took the radio call.

Constable Wood parked the police van in front of the gates to the church and got Mr Ted out from the back, putting him on his lead as he jumped down. They stood there and listened for a few minutes. They could hear nothing except for the gentle breeze blowing through the branches of the old oak tree that had stood at the church gate for about a hundred years; otherwise it was very quiet. The policeman thought to himself that if the old oak tree

155

could talk it could probably tell a thousand tales of all the comings and goings at the church over the years as families attended christenings, weddings and funerals, as it stood watch over the arched gateway where people passed through beneath its branches.

Constable Wood, knowing that at least twenty people had telephoned the police headquarters, thought he had better stay a bit longer and at least look around with Mr Ted.

"It seems quiet enough now Ted. But there must be something in this for so many people to ring the police. Let's have a look in here first."

He opened the gate to let himself and Mr Ted through, just as he did so they both heard an owl hoot in the tree above them. Constable Wood shone his torch up into the tree and he and Mr Ted looked up to see a tawny owl looking down at them. Mr Ted looked at Constable Wood before walking through the gate.

"That's not what we're looking for Ted. It's just an owl."

As they moved away from the gate and deeper into the graveyard the owl stopped hooting and all was quiet again. Constable Wood let Mr Ted off his lead and set him to work searching amongst the gravestones. Although they didn't really know what they were looking for, Mr Ted went off ahead with his nose to the ground looking for any unusual scent that he could find. Constable Wood followed keeping his eyes and ears open for anything out of the ordinary too. The graveyard was a spooky place in the dead of night, there was not a sound to be heard and all there was to look at was the church walls and the graves all around them. It made Constable Wood feel just a little bit uneasy, especially as he had been told that the villagers thought the screams were coming from the graveyard, but Mr Ted looked as if he was all right, moving from one grave to another, in and out of the head stones, busy searching for anything unusual.

They had searched most of the graveyard and done three sides of the church and had just turned the corner to do the last side when Mr Ted stopped in his tracks looked up and started barking, looking around for Constable Wood at the same time. He wanted to alert him to what he could see. He was looking at was a giant man dressed in white flowing robes, standing perfectly still in the cold moonlight. He was white all over, white clothes, white face and white hands. He wasn't moving at all, not even as Mr Ted got closer to him and started to circle around him.

Constable Wood ran towards Mr Ted to see what the fuss was about and he could see in front of Mr Ted a giant white marble angel standing over an old grave. He was walking quickly between the graves to get to Mr Ted.

"Ted, that's just a statue. Leave it. It's all right."

As he got to the grave being guarded by the marble angel he took hold of Mr Ted's collar and turned to walk him away. Just as he turned the ground opened up beneath him and he fell into a deep damp hole! He let go of Mr Ted as he fell. His foot landed on what he thought was wood, because of the sound it made in the dark as his foot went through it. He let out a scream as he fell. First at the shock of falling in a hole and then because his foot hurt as it burst through the wood. He was stuck firm and he couldn't pull his foot out. The more he tried the more the wood seemed to tighten around his ankle. He let out another loud scream as the splinters dug into his leg.

He looked out of the hole to try and get his bearings. His foot was firmly stuck in the wood, and above him he could see the giant marble angel looking down on him, and so too was Mr Ted. He realised he was in a grave, and stuck fast.

"Blimey Mr Ted, we were sent here to investigate reports of someone screaming. The only noises I've heard so far are what we've created ourselves, what with you barking at a marble angel and me screaming in this grave, there will be more phone calls to headquarters, and then what will we tell them?"

Constable Wood tried once more to pull his foot free. As he did so he took his torch from his pocket and shone it down towards his feet. He knew he was in a grave, but he was shocked at what he saw underneath him. In the light of the torch he could see that he had fallen into a freshly dug grave. There was a mound of earth at the side, and Mr Ted was stood on it looking down at him. In the bottom was a coffin, and he had one leg on it and the other in it. On a plaque screwed into the lid of the coffin were some words, he brushed away the dirt and he was able to read them, *Rest in Peace. Daniel Martin 1882 – 1962.* This man has been buried here for years he thought and the wood is rotting, but he wondered why his grave was open. Anyway, why it was open was not the most important thing on his mind right now; that was how he was going to get his foot out of the coffin and himself out of the grave. Mr Ted was pacing around the grave looking down on Constable

Wood; it didn't look like he could help much to get his stricken master out of the grave.

"Come close Mr Ted. Let me take hold of your collar."

Mr Ted leaned into the grave; Constable Wood took hold firmly and told Mr Ted to pull back. Constable Wood hung on to Mr Ted with one hand and used his other hand and his free leg to pull with Mr Ted. Slowly they managed to pull him upwards a little. Constable Wood felt his foot coming out of the coffin, and once it was free he soon scrambled over the top of the grave with Mr Ted's help, he pulled himself upright, letting go of Mr Ted at the same time. He shone his torch back into the grave and could see the hole he had made in the old coffin, and there staring up at them both was the skeleton face of Daniel Martin with its grinning teeth looking back at them both.

"Sorry about that Mr Martin. It was an accident!"

Then, over the radio came a call from police headquarters.

"Control to Alpha 41."

"Go ahead."

"We are getting more calls from the village. They are saying that there have been more screams coming from the church grave yard. Have you heard them?"

"No. It's all quiet here. I'm in the church yard now and we haven't heard any screams." he said with his fingers crossed behind his back.

He had just finished speaking on his radio to headquarters when a voice came from the angel.

"What are you doing here?"

Constable Wood looked startled and Mr Ted started barking again. He ran towards the angel, barking even louder as he went.

The voice from the angel said, "Stop him. It's only me."

The Reverend Jameson, vicar of All Saints Church walked into view alongside the angel.

"What's going on? I'm the vicar here and I live in the vicarage next door. All your barking and shouting has woken me up."

"We're here investigating reports of someone screaming in the village. Several people have telephoned to say they can hear screams."

"So did I. But I thought it was you and that dog. Did I see you climbing out of that grave? What were you doing in there?"

"I fell in it, there's an old coffin in there. Why is the grave open?"

"There's a funeral here first thing in the morning, it's a relative of Daniel Martin. That's his grave and they are going to be buried there too. We don't often get policemen running around our graveyard in the middle of the night so we thought it would be safe to leave it like that overnight."

"Well I've broken Daniel's coffin when I fell in there. Sorry about that."

"Don't worry. We'll put that right tomorrow."

Constable Wood said goodnight to the vicar, apologised again and led Mr Ted out of the graveyard and back onto the road. They still hadn't found the cause of the screaming noises that had awoken so many of the villagers; they hadn't heard it for themselves either. They set off along the road that runs through the rest of the village walking side by side with Mr Ted back on his lead. On the way along the road Constable Wood kept his eyes and ears open listening out for anything that sounded remotely like a scream. They must have been in the village for at least three quarters of an hour by now. They walked around the outside of the two pubs that were opposite each other near a small village green. Next they looked into the front gardens of the houses that were scattered along the road. When they got to a house called The Red House a black cat walked out of the drive straight into the path of Mr Ted. The cat took one look at Mr Ted, arched its back and hissed at him, spun around and leapt up onto a high wooden fence to get away and disappeared over the other side. Mr Ted pulled on his lead.

"Leave it Ted. He's gone now."

Constable Wood thought to himself that cats sometimes make screaming noises at night, especially if they are fighting each other, but that cat didn't scream, nor were there any signs of any other cats, yet. Anyway, most people knew that cats sometimes screamed at night, but no one mentioned that it might be cats in their phone calls to police headquarters; they were all saying that it sounded like human screams.

The pair walked a little further along the road. The road turned back on itself around a row of houses and back towards the church when they came across the opening to Pond Farm. There was no gate at the front of the farm entrance where it met the road. Constable Wood could see that there was an enclosed animal yard with buildings on three sides and a fence and gate on the other side. Outside the yard there was a large lawn and a small duck pond. When Constable Wood shone his torch around he could see some ducks alongside the pond on the bank, but they looked like they were asleep. The pair moved into the yard opening the gate then closing it quietly behind them. Looking out of one of the buildings was a horse, just like Churchill the police horse, they could have been brothers. The horse looked their way and snorted to acknowledge their presence, then turned around and went deeper into the darkness of his stable. Constable Wood noticed an opening into a larger building, nearly as big as a barn. Inside there was lots of hay stacked in bales one on top of the other, in the roof of the barn he could just make out a loft. They started to walk into the barn when Mr Ted stopped dead and wouldn't go any further, he looked up at Constable Wood and looked forward again into the darkness. The hair on his back stood up straight, something was there in the darkness and Mr Ted could smell it or see it, but whatever it was Constable Wood had no idea.

They stood in the opening for a moment or two listening for any sound or any movement. Then, suddenly and without any warning, there came the most ear piercing scream which made Mr Ted bark and Constable Wood jump with fright. It sounded to Constable Wood like a woman screaming for help, but help from what he didn't know. He shone his torch around the barn and couldn't see anything that gave him a clue as to what or who was screaming or why. Then again, as suddenly as the first scream came the second, but this time Constable Wood got a fix on where it was coming from, it was high up in the loft.

Mr Ted looked in the direction of the scream just for a moment but returned his gaze to the back of the barn at ground level. He was growling now, a deep mean growl of a dog ready to attack. Constable Wood shone his torch towards the back of the barn but could see nothing but hay stacked there.

"What is it Ted? What have you found?"

Then there came a third scream, much more piercing than the first two. A real cry of pain echoing around the barn and out into the night air, but there was no other sound. No sound of a struggle, no sound of a fight, no voices, no banging, no nothing. Still Mr Ted was fixing his gaze to the back of the barn floor. Constable Wood thought this was all very strange. There were screams coming from the loft, but Mr Ted was mainly interested in whatever was hiding at the back of the barn behind the hay. First things first thought Constable Wood, me and Mr Ted had better tackle whatever this is on the ground then get to the screams.

They moved forward, and he slipped Mr Ted off his lead to give him a free run inside the barn. If someone was hiding in there Mr Ted would flush him out.

"Seek Ted."

Now that he was free from his lead Mr Ted set off towards the back of the barn. He hadn't gone more than twenty paces into the barn when he was met by a bushy tailed fox coming towards him. Mr Ted growled. The fox bared his teeth in defiance. The fox was much smaller than the police dog and he knew it, he gave Mr Ted a wide berth and ran for the opening and freedom. He ran straight past Constable Wood looking back over his shoulder only once as he fled into the darkness outside. Mr Ted watched him go. That cleared the problem of what had been hiding in the barn.

Foxes sometimes scream at night thought Constable Wood to himself, but not like the screams they had heard coming from the loft. Just as he was thinking that another shriek came from the loft above them followed by the sound of something moving. Constable Wood shone his torch into the air and there above him perched on the edge of the loft were a pair of peacocks, screaming. They sounded very much like a human scream!

"That's it Mr Ted, we woke up an owl, we thought we had seen a ghost in the graveyard that turned out to be a marble angel, I fell in poor Daniel Martin's grave and broke his coffin, we woke up a vicar, frightened a cat, chased a fox in the search for the source of reports of screaming. Well we found the screaming in the end, and probably that old fox was thinking of having one of those birds for his dinner until you chased him out. So some good has come out of this caper, and what a relief that no-one was being attacked."

Mr Ted looked up at him with a knowing look in his eye and off they walked back to the dog van.

Chapter Fifteen

Poachers in the Woods

Constable Wood and Mr Ted spent lots of their time on patrol in the van. To Mr Ted it was like his second home, when he wasn't in the police dog kennels he was in the van and he liked it that way. In his mind the van was just as much his property as his kennel and he defended his territory every time anyone came near it by barking at them, until Constable Wood told him to be quiet. Sometimes he would growl quietly under his breath if he saw someone walking past, just to let Constable Wood know he had seen someone.

They were parked one night in Hawkridge town centre. It was getting late but there were still a lot of people about and Mr Ted was watching them out of the back window or through the hatch behind Constable Wood's driving seat. Growling quietly at first and then breaking out into loud barking every now and then, depending on whether he liked the look of the latest passer-by or not. He was barking when the police radio in the van burst into life. It was police headquarters calling for Constable Wood and Mr Ted. Constable Wood could hardly hear his radio over the noise Mr Ted was making and he told him to be quiet.

"Say that again please."

"Will you please go to Old Farm, Eaton and meet other police officers at the entrance. The farmer reports poachers on his land,"

"Yes, will do, we're on the way and we'll be there in ten minutes."

"Please approach with caution. The farmer thinks he has heard shotguns being fired."

Constable Wood started the police van, turned on the blue light and sped off out onto the A166 towards Eaton. Mr Ted, as usual, could hear the motor of the light turning on the roof of the van, and could see the reflection of the revolving blue light bouncing off the buildings that lined the road out of the town. He knew they were off to catch criminals and he started to turn around and around in the back of the van, almost as fast as the blue light was turning. He was barking with excitement because he just knew he was going to get involved in something exciting!

Constable Wood got to the lay by on the road outside the entrance to the farm. He could see Sergeant Irons and three more constables. He parked the van, got out and talked to the sergeant.

"I'm glad you're here," said Sergeant Irons, "I've seen the farmer and he says he saw some lights coming from that square wooded area over there."

He pointed to a dark clump of trees about half a mile across the fields.

"He has some pheasants in there. Some are in a pen, but some are in the trees, and he thinks the lights he's seen are men who are poaching the birds. He thought he heard a shotgun too, as if someone was shooting at the birds. We haven't actually seen anyone yet, though."

Constable Wood suggested that he go with Mr Ted to the woods and see what he could find. He asked the sergeant to watch the outside of the woods on all sides, with the constables, and let him know if they saw anyone coming out. With the plan agreed, Constable Wood got Mr Ted from the van, put him on his lead and set off across the field towards the woods in the distance. The sergeant and the others surrounded the woods, far enough away from the trees so that they could see if anyone came out into the open.

When Constable Wood and Mr Ted got to within a hundred metres of the wood, he thought he could see the dark shape of something moving, from his left to his right, immediately in front of the woods. It was so dark against the trees that he couldn't be sure what he had seen, or if he had seen anything at all. He looked again, and there right in front of the tree line, were two men walking quickly one behind the other. It must be the poachers he thought to himself, who else could be wandering about in the woods in the dark and so late at night. Mr Ted had spotted the movement as well, and Constable Wood could see him staring intently into the darkness at the movement ahead of him. Constable Wood had to think quickly, if he didn't act straight away he might lose them. Then he remembered that he'd been warned that they might have a gun. But he thought they needed the gun to shoot birds, surely they wouldn't use it against a policeman. He decided to make it quite clear to the men that he was the police and that he had a police dog with him by shouting out at them to stay where they were, and that's what he did. But what happened next shocked him and put Mr Ted in great danger!

He shone his police torch towards the men and shouted at them.

"Stay where you are. It's the police!"

When they heard his shouts the two men stopped for a moment and he thought that were looking straight towards his light. Then they turned and ran together in the same direction that they had been walking. He shouted at them again.

"Stand still! I have a police dog and I will release him. Stay where you are, now!"

The two men stopped again and looked towards him, but then carried on running again.

"Stand still! I will release the dog!"

Mr Ted was barking now, the men must be able to hear him he thought, as he shouted one more warning. For the last time he shouted at the fleeing men.

"Stand still or I'll release the dog!"

Mr Ted was straining at the lead as he heard Constable Wood shouting at the men. He knew that he would be running after them any moment, and then he felt Constable Wood lean forward and with his right hand release the lead from him.

"Stop them Ted!"

Mr Ted took off across the field with the men firmly in his sight, they stood no chance against his speed, and even if they did go into the woods his super sense of smell would soon find two men, sweating and out of breath. There was no hiding place for them now that Mr Ted was loose!

Mr Ted was about half way between Constable Wood and the two men when he saw them stop and look towards him. One of the men held something up in his arms and pointed it towards Mr Ted. Then there was a flash from it followed straight away by the familiar noise of a shotgun being fired.

"Down, Ted! Down!"

Mr Ted dropped like a stone, lying as flat and as motionless as he could on the ground as the shot from the barrel of the gun whistled over his head and on towards Constable Wood fifty metres behind him. Constable Wood dropped to the ground a split second after Mr Ted.

"Incredible" he thought, "They've used the gun against us. I hope Ted is all right."

Mr Ted never took his eyes off the men. He saw them both leap one after the other into the trees and disappear from sight. Constable Wood got up and went to him. He checked him over as best he could in the dark to make sure that he was all right and hadn't been hit by the shot from the gun. He certainly wasn't acting as if he had been injured and Constable Wood didn't find any injury either. Mr Ted was all right.

"Did I hear a gun?" said Sergeant Irons over the police radio.

"Yes you did. Send for back up. I've seen two men, they've shot at Mr Ted, but he's all right. They've gone into the woods and we're going after them."

He put Mr Ted back on his lead and ran with him towards the spot where they had seen the two poachers go into the trees. Once they were there the pair of them stood for a while and listened. They could hear the two men making a lot of noise going through the trees and undergrowth, their bodies brushing against the trees and their feet kicking through the fallen leaves and undergrowth in the woods. What they couldn't tell was how far away they were, or which way they were going. Constable Wood knew they were trying to get away, and he knew that if he was quick to get behind them Mr Ted would find them in amongst the trees. He kept Mr Ted on his lead and let it out as far as he could and told him to seek.

Mr Ted put his nose to the ground and walked up and down for a few paces before picking up the trail of scent left by the men as they ran into the trees. He followed the trail, pulling on the lead and dragging Constable Wood along behind him. The scent was strong, winding around some trees where it was easy for him and Constable Wood to make their way. But very soon it led through some thick bramble and hawthorn bushes. Mr Ted needed to crouch low to get through, the bramble pulling at his fur as he edged forward. The same bramble and hawthorn pulled at Constable Wood's uniform as he was pulled along behind his dog. The bushes got so thick that Constable Wood was crawling on his hands and knees to keep up behind Mr Ted, as he did so the bramble cut into his face and hands. Mr Ted was pulling harder and harder, trying to move faster after the men ahead of him. The scent was so strong now that he didn't need to have his nose close the ground, it was all around him. Constable Wood could tell that Mr Ted was getting close; he was pulling so hard against his lead. He made Mr Ted stop for a moment and listened. Mr Ted was right; they were close by, so close that they could hear the men talking to each other. Constable Wood could even hear what they were saying.

"They're right behind us. We'll never shake them off."

Constable Wood still couldn't see them so he let Mr Ted take him a few paces further forward until they came to a clearing free from brambles and hawthorn, and they were able to stand upright again. Just as they did they could see the outline of the two men on the other side of the clearing; they were about ten metres in front of them. Constable Wood shone his torch on them. He could see that one of them was on his knees with the shotgun in his lap and the second man was standing alongside him carrying a big stick and a large bag.

"It's the police, stay where you are!"

The man who was standing turned on his heels and started to run, just as the kneeling man began to stand up and follow him. Constable Wood took the lead from Mr Ted and shouted.

"Stop them Ted!"

Mr Ted didn't need telling twice, he'd been after these two since before the gun went off in the field. He raced forward; the first man he went for was the man with the gun. He ran at him and jumped on his back bringing him and the gun crashing to the ground. Constable Wood was right behind him and kicked the gun out of the man's reach. He handcuffed the man to a tree as he told Mr Ted to go after the other one. Mr Ted looked back at Constable Wood once, as if making sure that he was all right, before taking off after the other man. He stood no chance. Mr Ted was on him in seconds. When he was near enough he launched himself at the running man taking hold of his right arm, the arm that was carrying the stick. The power and speed of the police dog brought the man to the ground begging for Mr Ted to release him.

"Put that stick down!" and the man obeyed immediately.

"Mr Ted – Leave!"

Mr Ted let go of the man's arm, barking at him as Constable Wood took hold of him and told him he was under arrest.

Constable Wood called the sergeant on his police radio and asked the other officers to join them in the clearing. He kept his torch shining so that they could find him easily. The sergeant and the other constables were soon there and found the man handcuffed to the tree and Constable Wood with the second man.

"We'll take these two now. What's in that bag?"

He picked the bag up and opened it. Inside he found four pheasants, still alive and none the worse for their ordeal.

"You two will go to prison for what you've been up to tonight."

He told the constables to take the men, and their belongings back to the police cars at the roadside. Constable Wood and Mr Ted followed behind until the poachers were inside the police cars and driven away.

"Well done again Mr Ted. We wouldn't have got those two without you." he said giving Mr Ted a hug as he got into the back of the dog van.

Chapter Sixteen

Mr Ted Visits the Golf Course, but not to play golf

A couple of weeks after the poaching case, in which Mr Ted had been shot at, Constable Wood and Mr Ted, were on patrol in their police van one sunny Sunday morning. Also on patrol in the van with them were Constable Tony Harrington and his dog Reno. Reno was a German Shepherd and trained just like Mr Ted. In fact, Reno had been a police dog for a couple of years longer than Mr Ted and had just as many arrests as Mr Ted; he was good, very good. Together they made a fantastic team. Constable Harrington was driving the van and the two police dogs were in the back. Mr Ted was behind Constable Wood and Reno behind Constable Harrington. It was quiet, and it had been quiet all morning. There was not much traffic about and not many people walking about either, but it was still early in the day, just after eight o'clock in the morning on a Sunday, it was usually quiet then.

Constable Harrington decided to drive along the A6 road towards the gates of Broughton House, where the Queen sometimes visited. He thought that it might be a good idea to let the two dogs run around in the parkland, just inside the mansion house gates to give them a bit of exercise. As they approached the gates a green Ford Transit van drove out quite fast and pulled across the road right in front of the dog van causing PC Harrington to brake hard. It turned right as it came out of the gates and drove past the police van. As it went past, Constable Harrington looked at the driver, and could see another man sitting beside him on the passenger seat. The driver looked straight at PC Harrington and the passenger looked down and covered his face with his hands.

"That's a bit odd" said Constable Harrington, "I don't like the look of those two."

He didn't know why he didn't like the look of them, but something told him that they had been up to no good. It wasn't just the bad driving, there was something else but he didn't know what.

"I'm going after them. Call headquarters and check out the number on that van. Let's see if it is reported as stolen."

He turned the dog van around in the entrance to Broughton House and drove off after the Transit. He just wanted to follow it until they had checked with headquarters. Constable Wood used the radio and called the police control room.

"Will you please check the number of a van we are following on the A6 towards Hawkridge. The registration number is EZT 4116?"

"Stand by Alpha 41. We'll check and call you back."

Constable Harrington continued to follow the Transit van. He dropped a gear and, putting his foot down further on the accelerator, increased his speed to match the Transit. The message came back from police headquarters that there was no information on the Transit van. That made the situation even more puzzling because the driver was going even faster as he turned left off the road towards Greybourne. As it sped around the corner it nearly left the road, bouncing off the bank on the driver's side before righting itself again and speeding down the lane, with the police van in pursuit.

Reno and Mr Ted were getting excited at the speed their van was going, they sensed that something was going on, and began turning around in the back of the van and barking. The hair coming off the two dogs was swirling around the van and covering the two constables. Constable Harrington decided that the Transit would have to be stopped and put on the blue light on top of the police van roof. He flashed his headlights at the Transit driver. All that did was make the driver of the Transit go even faster. It was clear now to the two policemen that it was not going to stop easily and that they were involved in a chase. What they didn't know was why the people in the van were trying to get away from them. They chased after them along the narrow lanes towards Greybourne when suddenly the Transit van pulled off the road into a driveway. Constable Harrington turned in after them and they sped past a sign on the driveway that read *Greybourne Golf and Country Club;* they were going onto a golf club!

Constables Harrington and Wood thought that it would come to a stop in the car park, but they were wrong! The driver crashed the van straight through a rustic pole fence covered in climbing roses, that were in full bloom, and sped off with bits of fence and rose bush hanging off it. They left behind them a hole in the fence that was wide enough for the police van to follow, and sped off across the grass in front of the club house and over the first tee.

Constables Wood and Harrington could see a golfer taking a swing at a golf ball, and he had to jump clear of the Transit as it sped past him! The police van, with its blue light flashing was following in the car park. The golfer threw his golf club down, put his hands on his hips in disgust and looked on in amazement at the spectacle playing out in front of him. This sort of thing had never happened at the golf club before; it was normally a peaceful place.

If there was any lingering doubt in the police officers' minds that the men in this van were up to no good then it was gone now. There could be no mistaking that the driver and the other man in the Transit were intent on getting away from the police. The question on Constable Wood's mind was why? What could they have done, why were they running?

Constable Harrington dropped the police van into a lower gear and sped through the hole in the fence and off past the golfer onto the fairway after the Transit van which by now was doing over sixty miles an hour on the grass and swerving from side to side as it went. After four hundred metres the Transit driver drove onto the first green and spun the van around on the neatly cut grass, turning one hundred and eighty degrees around the marker pole with its little yellow flag on the top, to face the oncoming police dog van. It stopped momentarily. The number one green had been carved to shreds by the wheels as it made the tight turn around the pole. As it stopped the police officers thought that the men in the van would get out and run, leaving the van behind. But the Transit started moving again. This time it was heading straight for the police van which was closing in on them fast. The Transit driver picked up speed heading straight at them. It was obvious he meant to frighten the policemen and try to scare them off, or he was going to crash head on into the police van!

The Transit was at least twice as big as the police van. Realising what was happening Constable Harrington slowed down. He got himself ready to take avoiding action. As the two vans closed in on each other Constable Wood was telling the police control room over the radio what was happening, hardly making himself heard above the noise of the two police dogs barking in the back behind him. He thought he could hear the control say that the

Transit had been seen speeding away from an armed robbery at a petrol station in Enmore. He also heard the word *shotgun*. He tried to get more information, but he couldn't hear above all the noise in the van. Anyway, something was to happen in the next few seconds that took his mind of the radio conversation.

The front of the Transit van loomed ever bigger as it got closer to the police van.

"He's going to ram us!" shouted Constable Wood.

"I know" said Constable Harrington "hang on!"

At the last second he swung the steering wheel hard to his right as he swerved to avoid a crash. But they crashed into the back of the police van as they past each other! The sound of metal against metal was deafening as the police van rocked from side to side on its wheels. Somehow it kept upright. The Transit driver turned full circle and came from behind the policemen, then deliberately crashed into their driver's side, putting a massive dent in the side of the van where Reno was standing. Constable Harrington sped forward to get away from the Transit. It caught up with them again and this time rammed the front of the police van; knocking off the front bumper and knocking out all the front lights.

The officers and the dogs inside were getting knocked from side to side. The dogs were barking louder than ever. Frightened, they were scraping at the van walls to get out. The police van's engine stalled. There was steam coming out from under the bonnet. When the criminals could see that the police van was crippled, they sped off down the fairway towards the second green. They thought they were getting away and so did Constables Wood and Harrington. Even the dogs couldn't help them chase after criminals getting away in a speeding van. Constable Harrington turned the ignition key and the engine burst into life.

"We're off again! Hold on I'm going after them!"

As they sped down the fairway they could see the Transit van speeding along apparently none the worse for the crashes. It looked like the driver was trying to find a way off the golf course. He was driving along a boundary hedge with a barbed wire fence marking the perimeter; he swung the van back into the golf course and towards the police van again.

"No! Not again!" said Constable Wood bracing himself against what he thought was sure to be another ramming. But no, the Transit turned full circle again and drove as fast as it could straight at the barbed wire fence. Then it drove straight through it without slowing down, sending broken barbed wire flying into the air like a whip. Constable Wood could see that there were some horses in the field on the other side, they were startled and started to run away from the Transit in all directions as it sped through their field. Constable Harrington followed keeping away from the horses as he went. Constable Wood saw something being thrown from the passenger window, he couldn't tell what it was, except that it was about a metre long and quite thin, it landed in some long grass as the Transit drove onwards towards a wooden five bar gate at the far end of the field. The horses were scattering all over the field as the Transit crashed straight through that gate too, without slowing down, sending splintered wood into the air behind it!

They drove the van straight across the lane in front of the gate; straight through another closed five bar gate on the other side and into a field with crops growing in it; all the time followed by the pursuing police van. Just inside the field was a giant water tank. It stood high up on a wooden tower As the Transit sped past the tower it went into a four wheel sideways skid and crashed into it. The water tank and all the water in it came crashing to the ground! But the Transit just got clear and drove on.

Constable Wood could see that some of the startled horses were running onto the golf course through the hole in the fence, and some were following them out onto the lane, running in both directions to get away. He looked into the lane as the police van sped straight across it and then looked forward again to see the water tower crashing to the ground in front of them, sending thousands of gallons of water spilling out to the ground and up over their van. It was like they had driven straight into a lake. They came to a sudden halt as the cold water hit the hot engine. There they were in the middle of all the water with no engine power; they could see the Transit speeding off again on the other side of the crop field. Constable Harrington hurriedly tried to restart his engine, but it just kept spinning around with no signs of sparking into life, it was just too wet.

"Blast!" said Constable Harrington over the noise of the barking police dogs. "It's no good we're not going to get going this time Eddie."

Just as he said it the two officers watched in disbelief as the Transit tried to leap across a wide ditch at the far end of the field. The front wheels cleared the metre deep water ditch, but the back wheels landed right in it, and there it stayed. The driver tried hard to break free, but the more he revved the engine the more the wheels sunk into the soft soil on the side of the bank. They were stuck too!

"We've got them now." said Constable Wood. "Let's get Mr Ted and Reno out of the back."

They both jumped out of the police van at the same time into ankle deep water all around them, they walked to the back to get Mr Ted and Reno, at the same time watching the men in the Transit. They saw them get out, split up and run off in different directions away from the policemen.

"I'll get the driver with Mr Ted. You go for the passenger with Reno."

"It's a deal. I'll let Reno go first."

189

He shouted after the passenger and told him to stop. When he took no notice of him he shouted again and warned him that he would let the police dog go. Again the man took no notice.

"He's had his chance. Stop him Reno!"

He sent the big German Shepherd off on a course to which there could only be one outcome, the man was going to be stopped. Reno took off, barking as he went. Constable Harrington ran off after his dog and watched as the fleeing criminal looked over his shoulder and saw Reno thundering after him.

"Stand still now!"

Reno caught up with him and circled around him, barking menacingly, getting closer and closer to the man as he went around him. Constable Harrington was soon there and told Reno to stand still. The trained dog did as he was told, but continued to bark as he watched the criminal being arrested.

While all this was going on Constable Wood and Mr Ted watched as the driver ran into a yard where there was a cluster of farm buildings. There was a store shed, an open Dutch barn, a closed barn with some farm machinery in it, a milking parlour, a row of stables and some chickens and ducks wandering about the place loose. They heard the chickens clutter fussily as the man went into the yard and disappeared from view. Once Constable Wood saw that the passenger was under arrest he let Mr Ted run off to the yard.

"Seek Ted."

Mr Ted knew he was on a man hunt, he had seen the man go into the yard, and all he had to do was use his training and his nose to find him. He'd work out how to deal with him once he found him. Mr Ted put his nose to the ground as he went into the yard; there was no sign of the man that he was looking for. Mr Ted had to rely on his searching skills, his acute sense of smell and intelligence to seek him out. The chickens and ducks scattered all over the place out of Mr Ted's way as he worked. He took no notice of them except, as he was trying to follow the scent of a man, the strongest scent he was getting was of chickens, cows and ducks, but in amongst all that confused scent there was the scent of the man.

Mr Ted followed it first into the doorway of the shed, then straight back out again and into the big Dutch barn. He searched around in there but his nose and the scent he was following took him outside again and onto the stone surface of the yard. There he got the strongest scent yet of the man in the air. He spun his head towards the door of the closed barn. Constable Wood saw him look and followed as Mr Ted ran to the door. Constable Wood opened it for him as Mr Ted pushed past him to get inside as quickly as he could. He searched all around the barn floor, in and out of the machinery that was standing there, and worked his way to the back wall. There, standing upright in front of him was the Transit van driver, the very person Mr Ted was looking for!

To Mr Ted he looked frightened and mean at the same time. There was no way out of the barn without getting past Mr Ted and the policeman standing behind him. Mr Ted started barking and Constable Wood was just about to start speaking when the man picked up a claw hammer that was lying on the floor and began to swing it wildly at Mr Ted.

"Come on dog. You don't frighten me. You want some of this, then come and get it!"

The hammer was getting closer to Mr Ted's head and he knew he had to move fast to keep out of the way. He ducked and dived, barking all the time and looking for his chance to strike.

Then it came, the hammer swung past Mr Ted's face one more time. It was still going past and upwards away from Mr Ted when he took off and, with his mouth open, he launched himself at his attacker. He grabbed the man's arm, the arm holding the hammer, and bit into him. He felt the pain immediately and screamed out, dropping the hammer at the same time.

"Get him off! Get him off!"

"Leave!"

Mr Ted let go at once but never stopped barking at the man as he watched for any sudden and threatening movement. Constable Wood stepped towards the man and past Mr Ted and took hold of him and placed him under arrest. He handcuffed him and walked him out of the barn, with Mr Ted watching carefully, back towards Constable Harrington and his prisoner.

When they saw their dog van it looked a mess. Both bumpers had gone, all the lights were knocked out, the body panels were all dented and scratched, and on top of that a lot of water had got inside from the water tower crash. Still, the radio worked and Constable Wood called the police control room, told the operator where they were and what had happened and asked for transport for them, the prisoners and the dogs. They didn't have to wait long until help arrived. Sergeant Fleming got there first with a big van, big enough to take them all. Other police officers arrived and they helped to round up the horses that had run into the road and the golf club. They got them back into their own field again.

Then Constable Wood and Mr Ted walked back to where they had seen the men in the Transit throw something out of their van during the chase. Eddie set Mr Ted to work again; this time looking for whatever it was that had been thrown away. Mr Ted put his nose to the ground and started searching, looking and smelling for anything that seemed out of place in the long grass. He twisted from side to side as he went and Constable Wood could hear Mr Ted taking in the scent around him through his nose. He soon found a bag, a cloth bag about the size of a carrier bag. He took hold of it in his mouth and took it to Constable Wood. The policeman took the bag and saw inside that it was full of money, quite a lot of money, and a couple of balaclava masks.

"That's a good boy Ted, well done, but you've not finished yet. We're still looking for a long thin object. Seek Ted. Seek."

Constable Wood encouraged Mr Ted to carry on searching in the grass, and Mr Ted carried on using his nose and working hard to find whatever might be hidden there. He covered quite a lot of ground in his searching, and then suddenly he got a strong scent of something lying in the ground and headed towards it. There it was about half a metre long, half of it wood and the other half metal. Constable Wood saw that Mr Ted had found something and quickly walked over to see what it was.

"Good boy Mr Ted. Leave this to me. Leave it."

He bent down and saw lying on the ground a double barrelled sawn off shotgun. He left it there and called over the police radio to tell headquarters that he had found a gun; probably the gun that had been used in the Enmore petrol station robbery. He also told them that Mr Ted had found what looked like the money that had been taken in the robbery too. The police control room told Constable Wood to leave the gun where it was and they would send out the CID and some forensic experts to recover it and check it for fingerprints.

Once the CID and forensic team arrived Mr Ted and Constable Wood went back to the police station with Sergeant

Fleming, and handed their prisoners over to the custody sergeant. Reno and Mr Ted were treated to a drink and some food and rest. The dogs knew they had done well. The two constables got showered and changed into clean uniform and they were ready again for the next adventure. But it would be a long time before their van would be ready for police work again.

Chapter Seventeen

It's Hell in Hawkridge Town when the Angels Visit

It took a couple of weeks for Mr Ted's van to be ready for the road again. It was recovered from the field at Greybourne on the same day as he and Reno caught the two armed robbers, but it was in no fit state to be driven. It needed to go to an accident repair specialists to get new body panels, new bumpers and lights, and then be re-sprayed in its original white colour. That took ten days. Then it was transported back to the police workshops in Hawkridge where the engine was stripped and repaired after the cold water had damaged it when the water tower came crashing down. When that was done the police badges and lettering were applied to the bodywork, and then it was ready looking new, clean and as good as the first day it went on patrol.

Constable Wood put Mr Ted into the back of the van on its first day back with them. Mr Ted looked very pleased to get it back. He liked that van very much. Constable Wood drove them both to the police headquarters where they joined up with a lot more police officers for a briefing on a public event that was due to take place in Peace Park in Hawkridge later that day. When they got to the headquarters car park Constable Wood saw the big horse transport lorry parked there and several horses and their riders were gathered nearby ready to be loaded up. He got Mr Ted out from the van, put him on to his lead and walked him over to where the police horses were, hoping to meet up with Churchill and Constable Georgina Kennedy. Sure enough they were both there and Mr Ted spotted his old pal Churchill and pulled on his lead to get closer to him. The big grey horse lowered his head to Mr Ted's level and the two seemed to be talking to each other, Churchill let out a neigh and a snort and Mr Ted barked a little excitedly and wagged his tail. Constable Wood spoke to Georgina, "Are you here for this public order briefing Georgina?"

"I certainly am looks like it's going to be a big one to get all of us here."

After a while they put the animals away safely and went to join all the other police men and women in the briefing room.

Superintendent Pickett was in charge and he began the briefing by letting them all know that there was going to be a gathering at Peace Park of five hundred Hells Angels from the English Chapter of Hells Angels, all on their motorbikes. They were going to be joined by another five hundred Hells Angels who were travelling from the French Chapter. They were going to have a party celebrating the thirtieth anniversary of the creation of the English Chapter of their organisation. Whenever such large numbers of Hells Angels had gathered together in public in the past, whilst they all had a good time, there was always the potential for trouble and the possibility that they could end up fighting each other or fighting local youths who might be looking for trouble the superintendent warned. Also, it just so happened that there was the annual fun fair in the park at the same time, which always attracted large numbers of people from all over the area. Then, to cap it all, the Mayor was holding a civic reception in the Museum that was in a large building in the park quite near to where the fairground was. The superintendent went on to say that there was going to be three hundred civic dignitaries and business people at the reception and civic ceremony. It was going to be a busy day whatever happened and the Superintendent told them to patrol the area and keep the peace. There was no need for everyone to be on patrol in the park at the same time, but they should take it in turns and in small numbers and only be there all together if any fighting or other disturbance broke out that required police intervention. Once the briefing was over the police officers, including the dogs and horses, made their way to a holding area in a part of the park that was closed off and behind a high fence out of sight of everyone else.

By the time most of the police men and women got into the park the funfair was open and doing brisk business. The Hells Angels were starting to arrive in convoys on their motor bikes and they began setting up a stage area for a band. The fairground ride music competed with the music of the band and the crowds of people at both events were having a good time, until that is another unexpected group of motor cycle riders rode their machines into the park.

They started mingling with the Hells Angels and it became clear that they were not welcome. Not that anyone was fighting, but arguments broke out and some of the bikers looked pretty angry with each other. Constable Wood and Mr Ted were in the park; Constable Kennedy was there too with Churchill and some other police horses and riders. There were some other police officers too amongst the crowd at the Hells Angels event and in the fairground.

Constable Kennedy could see right over the heads of everyone there as she sat on top of Churchill. As she looked towards the fair, and the bright lights and music of the fairground rides, she saw several of the Angels arguing. It was starting to look nasty. She rode Churchill over towards the arguing people when she saw several hundred more people dressed in motor cycle clothing, carrying sticks and iron bars, running into the park from the road. It was obvious they were going to attack the Angels and she called over the police radio for more police officers to join her.

The fighting soon broke out right in front of her. On her own she was powerless to do anything about it. The fight was in full swing by the time police reinforcements got there a couple of minutes later. People were hitting each other with sticks, bars and fists, and it seemed as if the English and French Chapters of the Hells Angels were being attacked by another motor bike gang. The police horses, including Churchill, rode through the fighting mob and separated them into two groups and the fighting stopped for a while, but they had to be kept apart somehow.

The horses and their riders kept the Hells Angels to one side as Constable Wood and Mr Ted, with six more police dogs and handlers, kept the other group away by forming a line in front of the crowd. Mr Ted and the other dogs were barking and that was enough to keep the angry mob away from the police line. Constable Kennedy could see that people were injured, and she could see that some still carried the sticks and iron bars that they had come with. For a time the standoff looked very ugly and uneasy. People in the crowd on both sides were baiting and threatening each other, but the combined presence of police dogs and horses seemed to be working for the moment.

Using his police radio, "What can you see Georgina?" asked Constable Wood.

"It looks like the people at the back of the crowd are moving towards you."

"Which crowd Georgina?"

"Not the Hells Angels, the others."

As she finished speaking the bikers started throwing things at each other, over the police officers and at each other. Stones, sticks and bottles came raining down on the crowd from both sides. Then, without warning fireworks were thrown at the police horses, thunder flashes, bangers and flares. Then more bottles and stones were being thrown at them all. Churchill was hit on the head and his back by flying stones and bottles, so was Constable Kennedy. A thunder flash exploded at Churchill's feet but he stood his ground, even though he looked startled. It was very frightening for the animals and the police.

The crowd started closing in on each other pushing forwards against the police lines. The dogs were barking and snapping at those that were hitting them and their handlers, and the horses were pushing against the Hells Angels to try and keep them back. Two men got close to Churchill and Constable Kennedy and hit out at him with some sticks they were carrying. Churchill tried to move away from the attack as the men carried on hitting him, harder with each blow. Startled and hurt, he reared up on his hind legs as he screamed out in pain. Constable Kennedy was unseated and fell backwards off her horse, landing with a thud on the ground beneath her. Churchill was rider less. Constable Kennedy had dropped the reins and Churchill was loose and vulnerable.

With the breath knocked out of her body shocked by the fall, Constable Kennedy was struggling to stand up and get back to him. Still the thunder flashes, stones and bottles rained down from above. Before she could get up properly, two Hells Angels grabbed her and pulled her into their midst.

One of them tormented her, "What are you going to do now little lady? Not so big when you're not on that beast are you?" as they pushed her between each other menacingly.

Constable Wood had seen what happened to Georgina, and he could see that Churchill had been attacked and was loose. He moved forward with Mr Ted towards where he had last seen Georgina. He got to Churchill first and took hold of his reins.

"It's all right boy, we'll sort this mess out in a minute."

Churchill recognised Mr Ted and Constable Wood straightaway and lowered his head to Mr Ted glad to see his friend. Constable Wood passed Churchill's reins to another police horseman and continued with his search for Georgina in the crowd. He couldn't see or hear her from where he was. The crowd was far too dense for that. He looked up at one of Georgina's colleagues who sat astride on top of a black stallion.

"Can you see Georgina? Where is she?"

"Yes, I can see the top of her head over there about fifteen metres into the crowd. She's being hit and pushed around."

Constable Wood pushed forward into the crowd with Mr Ted barking and snapping at the heels of everyone who got in his way and wouldn't move. Ted cleared a path straight to Constable Kennedy. What they didn't know was that they were being followed through the crowd by Constable Tony Harrington and his police dog Reno. They both got to Georgina at the same time and Constable Wood shouted to the men in front of him.

"Leave her alone, let go now!"

Mr Ted and Reno were barking aggressively and trying to bite the men who had hold of Georgina. The men pushed the policewoman towards Constable Wood. He wanted to arrest them, but they had enough to do in the crowd looking after themselves and getting back out again, without taking someone into custody. Constable Wood did get a good look though at the man who had been holding Georgina. He looked like most of the bikers, dressed as he was in black leather, but he stood out from the others because he had ginger hair and a thick ginger beard, and on top of that he had a black patch covering his right eye! You could not mistake him if you saw him again, and Constable Wood hoped he would see him again sometime.

Constable Harrington and Constable Wood stood back to back with Mr Ted and Reno on their leads out in front of them barking at the crowd. Georgina Kennedy was in between her two police colleagues, as the dogs created a space in the crowd for them to get back out safely. They got Constable Kennedy back to Churchill and she quickly remounted him. He was pleased to see her safe and back up on his back.

"Thank you Eddie and you Mr Ted."

Once she was safely rescued from the crowd, the horses and dogs, in a joint operation, charged the fighting mob and split them up in all directions, and kept splitting them up until it wasn't a crowd anymore and the fighting had stopped.

There was still some shouting and baiting from some of the bikers as they went back to their bikes and the odd thunder flash was thrown at the police, but nothing like the fighting that had gone on before. Eventually all the bikers had left on their machines, and apart from the fair, which was still in full swing as if nothing had happened at all, the park returned to a sense of normality. The police officers returned to their holding base as Churchill and Constable Kennedy were checked out for any injuries that they might have had. They were both a bit bruised and shaken, but apart from that they were fit and healthy, much to everyone's relief. With the Hells Angels gone there was no real need for most of the police men and women, or the horses and dogs, in the park any more, but the Superintendent kept most of them there for a while longer just in case the bikers came back or started fighting again somewhere else.

"What I want you to do is patrol the park, including the fair and the Mayor's reception. Just make sure everything is as it should be please. Constable Wood, will you go out first in your van? I'll send a couple of foot patrols around the fair ground."

Constable Wood went out to his van with Mr Ted and off they went on a tour of the park eventually ending up in the car park outside the museum. There was no sign of the Hells Angels or anyone else wanting to cause any trouble and so Constable Wood thought that he could safely stay in the car park for a while. He got Mr Ted out of the police van and together they walked amongst the quiet of the trees that surrounded the museum reflecting on the day's events. Inside the museum the Mayor's reception was in full swing, and from where he was standing Constable Wood could see people talking to each other in the tranquil surroundings of the museum's conference room. This was a totally different scene from the bikers' fight that had happened earlier a couple of hundred metres away.

"That's more like it" thought Constable Wood to himself, "why can't people behave like this all the time when they meet in public?"

He could see the mayor inside, and other councillors that he recognised, they all seemed to be enjoying the event, and seemingly unaware of all the trouble that there had been. The quiet of the car park was disturbed by the appearance in the driveway of the mayor's black Rolls Royce civic car driven by the council's long serving chauffeur. The big car turned into the car park and majestically drew to a dignified halt outside the front door to the museum. The chauffeur got out and walked into the building, although Constable Wood couldn't hear it because it was so quiet, he could see that the car's engine was still running by the small amount of grey smoke that was coming out of its exhaust pipe at the back of the car.

"That's a bit risky," thought Constable Wood, "leaving the car running like that with no one in it."

He started to walk with Mr Ted towards the gleaming black limousine, when Mr Ted started to growl when he saw, coming around the side of the building, a man dressed in motor cycle clothing, but it wasn't just any man! Constable Wood recognised him immediately. He stood out with his ginger hair, thick ginger beard and the patch over his eye.

"Stay where you are. I want to talk to you."

When he saw Constable Wood and Mr Ted he ran towards the Rolls Royce, jumped in to the driver's seat, selected the drive gear and drove off with the wheels spinning on the loose gravel ground beneath him. He had to turn the car around to get out on to the road, and he drove at Constable Wood and Mr Ted as he was turning the huge car around in one forward movement. Constable Wood shouted at him to stop but the biker sped past him and out onto the road leaving Constable Wood and Mr Ted standing there in amazement at the sheer cheek of it all.

He wasted no time getting back to his van, putting Mr Ted into the back he sped off after the mayor's car. On the way he radioed into his police control room and told them what he had seen and that he and Mr Ted were chasing after the limousine. As he pulled out onto the road he could just see the back of the Rolls Royce as it sped away in front of him. He followed it along Old Enmore Road until it got to the traffic lights with Copingstone Road where Constable Wood saw it go around a small queue of cars waiting for the red traffic signal to turn green. The Rolls Royce went through the red light without stopping and turned right, up the long steep hill of Copingstone Road. By the time

Constable Wood got to the lights they had turned green and he tuned up the hill after the Rolls.

He used his police radio to tell the control room which way they were going and asked if the road ahead could be blocked somewhere. The Rolls Royce with its six and half litre engine was leaving the pursuing little police van further and further behind as it sped along the Enmore Road towards the county boundary. By the time Constable Wood drove around the big roundabout in Slipsley on the eastern outskirts of Hawkridge he could just make out the back of the Rolls Royce on the dual carriageway road that opened out ahead of him. He was never going to catch it now he thought.

"It looks like he's getting away, and I'll never know who he is" he thought as he pressed the accelerator pedal to the floor.

He couldn't get any more speed out of the van no matter what he did. Mr Ted was in the back barking and turning around and around, waiting for his chance to get out and after the ginger bearded man who had attacked Constable Kennedy. Just when he thought there was no hope, Constable Wood saw two police Range

Rovers across the road ahead of them, their blue lights flashing, blocking it just at the entrance to Upperidge Park.

"Good! They'll stop him."

He watched as the speeding Rolls Royce skidded hard and swung onto the central reservation that split the two sides of the dual carriageway road and drove past the Range Rovers, turning right in to the park, past the iron gates that were standing open and onto the long drive that led eventually to the big house at the end of it. Constable Wood followed the course of the Rolls Royce into the park. He could see the big car slowing down. It was heading for a dead end. There was no way out for the car except back the way it had come. To do that the thief had to somehow get past a police dog van that was closing in on him and two police Range Rovers that were now blocking the gates. He couldn't drive around them now; there was no room for that.

The car stopped and the driver's door flew open as the ginger haired, one eyed man leapt from it and ran towards the fields at the side of the road. All that was between him and freedom he thought was the wooden fence around the field and the police dog. If he could clear the fence and get away from the dog he'd be home free, or so he thought.

"This one's yours Mr Ted; he's played right into our hands. His six and half litre engine can't help him now."

Constable Wood brought the police van screeching to a halt and ran around the back to let Mr Ted out. Mr Ted was already watching the man running and was barking as Constable Wood shouted, "Stop him Ted!" Mr Ted went after him until he got so close that he could almost feel Mr Ted's hot breath on his back. Mr Ted took off and in full flight; he hit the man in the small of his back with his front paws. His weight and speed knocked the breath out of the man and knocked him down to the muddy wet ground, flat on to his face. He rolled on to his back just in time to see Mr Ted climb on to him and put his nose and mouth right into the man's face and bark at him, holding him there pinned to the ground until Constable Wood caught up with them. The hot breath of the police dog against his face made the man tremble with fear, fear that he was about to be bitten in the face by the big police dog.

"Leave him Ted!"

Mr Ted stopped barking and moved away from the man.

"Are you going to come quietly?"

"Yes, just keep that dog away from me."

"All right then. Get up slowly. No sudden moves and he won't hurt you."

The man started to get up, but as soon as he was upright he took a swing at Constable Wood catching him with a blow with his clenched fist to the officer's shoulder. Mr Ted reacted at once and leapt at him taking hold of his right arm in a vice like grip. He tried to shake Mr Ted off but his bite got even harder until the man started to scream in pain.

"I told you. Stand still and I'll get the dog off you!" said Constable Wood angrily.

The man did as he was told and Constable Wood told Mr Ted to leave him alone. Constable Wood handcuffed him and put him in to a compartment in the back of the police van, alongside Mr Ted, and drove back to the police Range Rovers at the gates.

"We've got him." he told the waiting policemen. "Will one of you take the Rolls Royce back to the museum please? The keys are in it."

Constable Wood and Mr Ted took their prisoner back to the police station and booked him in with the cell block sergeant. There he told the sergeant all about the assault on Constable Kennedy in the park, and how he saw the same man steal the mayor's Rolls Royce and the chase that followed.

"You'll be staying here for quite a while." said the sergeant as the ginger haired man was led away to the cells.

Constable Wood went to the police canteen and found Constable Kennedy sitting there. They had a cup of tea each as Constable Wood told he the story of how Mr Ted had caught the man who had assaulted her in the park.

"I want to go and thank him" said Constable Kennedy, "and I think Churchill will want to as well."

They walked out into the police station yard where Churchill was standing next to the horse lorry. Constable Wood got Mr Ted from the police van and the two animals greeted each other. Mr Ted did it with a bark and by a wagging tail, and Churchill did it by lowering his head towards Mr Ted and snorting at him.

"Thank you Mr Ted. You're a brilliant police dog, and we love you."

Chapter Eighteen

Mr Ted goes down Memory Lane

Constable Wood had always promised John Edwards, the Hawkridge milkman who had so kindly and reluctantly given Mr Ted to the police force for training as a police dog all that time ago, that he would one day return with Mr Ted so that he could see how he had developed in the police. Constable Wood drew up outside John's house one Sunday and parked in the road. John Edwards, his wife and children, came out from their house as the policeman was proudly getting Mr Ted from the back of the patrol van. Mr Ted wasn't on his lead as he jumped down from the back of the van, he saw the family straight away and recognised them at once, he rushed towards them but Constable Wood shouted "Down Ted!" and Mr Ted obeyed by lying still on the ground before them wagging his tail.

"How did you do that?" asked John, "I would have thought he might run off down to the field with the horses just like he used to."

"I told you he could be trained," said Constable Wood. "Watch this."

Then he and Mr Ted put on a display of dog obedience right there in the street in front of the Edwards family, and they were all amazed at the spectacle. Mr Ted obediently walked off his lead at Constable Wood's side, up and down, around and around. Staying when he was told, and coming to Constable Wood every time he was asked.

"That's very impressive." agreed the Edwards all at once.

"That's not all, let me tell you about the things he's done since we saw you last. You won't believe all that he's been involved in. He's made a couple of friends, a dog called Baker and a horse called Churchill. He's met a giant snake; he's rescued some missing and vulnerable people, arrested lots of people, and met The Queen and her corgi. Pretty active wouldn't you say?"

"Bring him in and let's talk some more."

Mr Ted ran up to the Edwards family, wagging his tail with excitement at seeing them all again. He never once tried to run across the road to the field like he had done so many times before. They all made a great fuss of him, Mr Ted even rolled onto his back as they rubbed his tummy.

Over a cup of tea inside the family house Constable Wood said, "We've got to go to a special ceremony at the Crown Court. Judge Moss wants to see Mr Ted, he keeps seeing criminals at the court that Mr Ted has had a hand in catching, and I think he is going to be presented with a certificate. It's in two weeks time and we can invite some guests, would you like to come?"

"Would we like to come? You try and keep us away."

Two weeks later, with Mr Ted brushed and groomed with extra special care until his coat shone, he wore a brand new collar and lead. Constable Wood wore his best uniform neatly pressed with highly polished shoes as they entered Court number one at Hawkridge Crown Court. Sitting in the public gallery were the Edwards family, looking on as Constable Wood and Mr Ted presented themselves in front of the red robed judge sitting high above them.

"I have asked for you to come here today so that, on behalf of the public of Walthamshire, I can thank you both for the outstanding work that you do together in protecting us all. I know a great deal about the criminal cases that you have been involved in, and there is no doubt that Mr Ted is a very capable and brave dog. Congratulations."

Judge Moss handed Constable Wood a certificate of commendation, shook his hand and said, "Well done to you both. I hope that you go on having many more exciting adventures. I look forward to receiving more criminals from you two."

Constable Wood and Mr Ted left the courtroom with looks of satisfaction on their faces to be greeted on the court steps by some reporters and cameramen from the local papers who wanted the story of the police dog and handler team who had been so successful in just one year in catching so many criminals and finding missing people.

"What next PC Wood?" they shouted.

"Whatever we get sent to, Mr Ted is ready for it." Constable Wood smiled and Mr Ted wagged his tail.

About the Author

Eddie Halling was born in South Wales and spent his childhood in Swansea before moving to England for work. He joined the Bedfordshire Police serving for thirty years in total. During his early police career he spent some time as a police dog handler working mainly in the south of the county with his police dog, Baron. It is this work that has inspired the author to write "Mr Ted's Police Dog Adventures", which are all based, at least in part, on his time and work as a police dog handler.

Printed in Great Britain
by Amazon.co.uk, Ltd.,
Marston Gate.